A

G000021913

Recent Titles by Aileen Armitage from Severn House

ANNABELLA

CAMBERMERE

JASON'S DOMINION

MALLORY KEEP

THE RADLEY CURSE

A WINTER SERPENT

A WINTER SERPENT

Aileen Armitage

This title first published in Great Britain 1999 by
SEVERN HOUSE PUBLISHERS LTD of
9–15 High Street, Sutton, Surrey SM1 1DF.
First published in the USA 2000 by
SEVERN HOUSE PUBLISHERS INC., of
595 Madison Avenue, New York, NY 10022.

British Library Cataloguing in Publication Data

Armitage,   Aileen
        A winter serpent
        1.   Romantic suspense novels
        I.   Title
        823.9'14 [F]

        ISBN 0-7278-5475-5

Printed and bound in Great Britain by
MPG Books Ltd, Bodmin, Cornwall.

FOR PETER

ONE

TANYA was determined to be seduced. One way or another she would prevail upon Gregory Efimovitch to make a woman of her, as he had done so many other girls in the village. No longer could she bear to be pushed aside out of the giggling circle of girls grouped about the village pump, rolling their big eyes, their broad shoulders shaking with gleeful pride. They hushed their whispers whenever Tanya squeezed closer to listen.

"Go away, Tanya," they would say, "you're not old enough to listen to women's talk."

Women indeed! Most of them were only about sixteen themselves, barely four years older than herself. But she had caught stray whispers of their excited chatter and from the snippets she had gathered enough to realise the cause of their excitement. One after another had fallen prey to Gregory Efimovitch's lustful hands, and far from being ashamed, they were proud to have been made into real women by this strong, virile youth, and more than one pretty wench hoped he might yet take her as his bride.

Sasha, one of the prettiest girls in Pokrovskoe, had blurted out her story this morning, her eyes shining with a radiance Tanya had never seen before. The other girls, entranced at Sasha's story, had been unaware of Tanya sitting silently near by under the pretence of taking a stone from her shoe.

"What was it like, Sasha? Tell us," they had demanded eagerly, and Sasha's face had taken on a far-away, rapt expression.

"I was coming home from the baker's, for my mother had sent me down for a loaf. Usually she will not allow me out once dusk falls, but there was no bread in the house, so I had to go. I was walking back, the loaf still warm under my arm, when suddenly—there he was."

"Gregory? Where? How did he look? What did he do?" the voices chorused, each eager to satisfy her own curiosity.

"It was by old Efim's barn. I saw no one as I approached, but suddenly Gregory was standing there in the half-light, smiling and leaning on the door post."

"What did he say to you?"

"Not a word. He just smiled for a moment and I stopped and stared. You know what eyes he has."

"Indeed!" Tanya listened. She knew what Sasha meant. Gregory Efimovitch's eyes were the most startling thing about him. He was tall and broad and strong, but no more handsome than any of the other village lads. His hair was long and straggly and usually ill-kempt, but his eyes . . . They were keen and blue and penetrating, so piercing that village folk said he could see right through you and into your very soul. She listened again to Sasha's soft voice.

"Then he moved in front of me and barred the way. I told him I must hurry home or mother would be angry with me, but he still just smiled that mocking smile of his."

Tanya could hear the girls' deep breathing as Sasha paused, a dreamy expression on her face as she recalled the meeting.

"He still said nothing. He just reached out and unbuttoned my bodice."

"That's just how he approached me," said Natasha quietly. She had never been the same since the night Gregory had seduced her. Her tomboy manner was gone and a new, womanly glow kept her aloof from the rest.

8

Katya clapped a hand to her mouth to stifle a shriek. "Didn't you slap him then?"

"No." Sasha's voice grew fainter. "He took the loaf from me and drew me into the barn. It was soft and warm in the hay." She paused.

"Well? And then?" Katya demanded breathlessly. "Tell us what he did then. Did he seduce you? Was he gentle?"

Sasha smiled. "No, not gentle. Rough and swift like a bull in the field, but it was so beautiful, so exciting."

Katya grunted. "He sounds like a savage to me. I would prefer more gentle wooing than that Gregory doles out. All the girls say he is rough."

Sasha laughed. "You're just jealous, Katya, because no one has made a woman of you yet. But your turn will come."

"Not with Gregory Efimovitch. He's too proud by half, thinking any village girl would be glad to tumble with him, but not me. I shall wait till I'm married. My mother says a wench isn't half so valuable as a wife once she's let herself be seduced, and I have my pride."

"Your pride and your virtue are intact—more's the pity," Sasha retorted, and then bit her lip. Tanya knew she was feeling sorry for taunting Katya who could not help her plainness. Natasha drew closer to Sasha. Even Tanya could detect the cameraderie that now existed between them, as objects of Gregory's lust. They were proud of it, a select little coterie from which mere virgins were excluded.

Tanya finished fastening her shoe and rose. Sasha's eyes brightened fiercely when she saw her. "Have you been listening, Tanya?" she demanded. "You wicked little eavesdropper! Don't you dare repeat what you've heard, you hear me?"

Tanya fled before the older girl might slap her. She had heard every word, but she wished she knew what it all meant. To be seduced sounded a very pleasant experience, and one

9

that gave a girl added poise and maturity. All the other girls respected one who had been seduced—especially if it was by Gregory Efimovitch. She was heartily sick of being treated as a child, by them and by Grandmother. Now if she could get Gregory to seduce her, then things would be very different.

She walked slowly down the hill from the church and along the road that led to Grandmother's cottage, the chickens scattering, squawking, before her as she walked. Beyond the village lay the river Tura and beyond its meadows the vast Siberian steppe with its fir and pine forests rolling away to Tobolsk and beyond. Pokrovskoe village was a tiny speck, so she had heard, in the limitless expanse that was Russia, but it was all the world she knew. And very little ever happened here. A birth or a death occasionally were the only highlights in an otherwise uneventful village life, and Tanya longed to become a woman and experience these wonderful, ecstatic new sensations that Sasha spoke of.

Grandmother was in the little cottage yard, scattering grain to the hens. "Where have you been, child?" she asked sharply. "Gossiping again?"

"No, Grandmother."

"But you're late. I'm having to feed the hens for you. Come now, you can't afford to be lazy and ignore your tasks. Here." She handed over the basket of grain, and Tanya took it. Grandmother eyed her curiously.

"What is it? What are you thinking about, child? I don't know, I never knew such a one for day-dreaming. You don't take after your mother at all."

Tanya knew it was a source of great disappointment to Grandmother. Mother had been bright and gay and always busy until childbirth had wrested her suddenly from her contented life. Grandmother had liked Father well enough till he

10

died of a sudden illness, but he had never measured up to the warmth and industry of her daughter in her eyes.

"Come on now, look alive," Grandmother urged. "What on earth are you moping about now?"

Tanya looked up at her. "I want to be a woman," she said simply. But she knew her grandmother would never understand.

Grandmother snorted. "It'll come soon enough, and then there'll be no going back. Worry and work, that's all being a woman means. Enjoy yourself while you're young, child."

Tanya tossed handfuls of grain to the hens sadly. There it was again—child, young. No one seemed to realise that at twelve she was on the very brink of womanhood and eager to talk to someone who would understand and help. Grandmother was kindly enough in her rough, abrupt way, but she had no understanding of how people felt, deep down inside. To her it was the external things that counted—being on time and reliable, paying bills when they were due, keeping the cottage clean and scrubbed and one's hair well brushed. There was no time for brooding or hoping in Grandmother's life. Everything depended on being always active and busy, working hard to make life work out right.

Already she was planning for the future, how to take care of Tanya in the event of her own death.

"After all, I'm well past sixty and I can't expect to live for ever," she would say. "And as you've no other kin to care for you, we must look for a good husband for you to marry as soon as you're old enough. In another five years, maybe, and then when I see you well settled with a hardworking young husband, perhaps I can die in peace."

Sometimes, on the rare occasions when Grandmother was in a contemplative mood, she would look up from scraping vegetables and say, "There's young Boris whose father has a well set-up farm. He's about four years older than you. What do you think of him? I know it's early days yet, but it's worth thinking about."

And now and again she would produce the name of another village lad, but never that of Gregory Efimovitch. Tanya wondered at the omission. One day when Grandmother was cataloguing possible suitors, Tanya timidly ventured his name. The effect was startling. Grandmother dropped her rolling-pin.

"That one!" she snorted. "You don't know what you're saying, child; I admit his father, Efim, is fairly well-to-do, with his own farm and he has worked hard in the past to make it pay, but his son is not for you."

"Efim is head man of the village, Grandmother."

"That's as may be, but his son has earned himself a dreadful reputation already, and him not eighteen years old yet. Do you know what he is nicknamed? Rasputin—the rake. And it's well earned, as I hear. There's not a more dissolute ne'er-do-well this side of St Petersburg. He'll make no one a decent husband, mark my words. No, he'll not do for you, child."

Grandmother scooped up the battered pastry, screwed it into a ball and began to roll it out again. Tanya could tell from her savage movements that she was angry, but determined to learn more about this fascinating youth. She lowered her eyes demurely.

"Surely his family is good enough for us, Grandmother? Not only is Efim head man, but he was once coachman in the Imperial Mail. I am sure the girls of the village would be happy at such a catch."

Grandmother grunted. "Aye, old Efim did well enough for himself, but he's gone downhill since his wife died. Drinks like a fish now, I hear, and doesn't take the same care to his work as he did. I reckon the devil has marked him out for misfortune, more's the pity, what with his wife dying, then his house burning down and two of the children dying so sudden like. No wonder the poor man drinks with naught left to show for his life but a lazy son like that Gregory."

"He's not lazy, Grandmother. He works hard as a wagoner. He's away for days at a time, the girls say, and it can't be an easy life."

"All the same, he's a ne'er-do-well and not for you, my lass. I don't know why you're so interested in him all of a sudden, but nice girls don't bother with the likes of that Rasputin, and that's a fact."

Grandmother set to rolling the pastry again in a way that indicated that the subject was closed. But Tanya went on thinking of the roistering young man who brought such a sparkle to the eyes of the bigger girls.

That night, in the little low-raftered bedroom, Tanya unbuttoned her frock and let it slip to the floor. In the piece of cracked mirror over the dressing-chest she surveyed herself critically. Was she pretty enough to catch Gregory's eye so that he might seduce her? Whatever Grandmother might say about him, Tanya was still determined to make him take her into the hay if she could, for until then the other girls would never accept her as one of themselves. It was a mark of dignity, a cachet of social acceptance to be one of his conquests, and attain that zenith of achievement she would, if it lay within her power.

The dark-eyed solemn little face in the mirror was pretty enough, she decided, and the long dark hair swept becomingly over her pale shoulders when she unpinned it from its plaits. But her figure! Even she could tell that its long, thin straightness was unlikely to tempt Gregory into reaching for her buttons. Sasha and Katya were deep-bosomed, wide-hipped girls like most of the village lasses, their ample figures bearing testimony to their fertile peasant vocation for child-bearing.

But not so the virginal thin body in the mirror. No matter how she pushed up her budding breasts, they resembled no more than mole-hills on the vast steppe.

Tanya sighed and pulled on her nightgown. It was tragic to be only twelve and still built like a child when her inner self was crying out for womanhood and fulfilment. But it was no use trying to talk to Grandmother about it, for she would never understand.

It was only as sleep was beginning to flicker at the edges of her consciousness that Tanya remembered that girl—what was her name?—who had been so elated after walking one evening on the riverbank with Gregory Efimovitch. He had made a woman of her—out of chivalry, perhaps, but nevertheless, he had—and she had been as flat-chested as any boy. So all was not lost yet. Perhaps, if he had time on his hands, he would seduce Tanya if she arranged matters so that the opportunity arose.

Seduction. What a lovely word it was! So thrilling, so romantic—so grown up. She smiled as she visualised herself being welcomed warmly into the select group around the village pump, one of them at last. But before she could wonder for long at the details of a seduction and what exactly happened, she was fast asleep.

TWO

OLD Efim sat on a chair by his cottage door, smoking his clay pipe and enjoying the last of the sunlight. Perhaps when the sun went down he could hope to see his son returning, but even of that he was not sure. Gregory came and went as he felt inclined these days. If he dallied with a wench in the meadows, it was not for old Efim to complain, for Gregory had had a mind of his own for a long time now, and little that his father said had any effect on him.

Efim sighed and stretched his legs. He was a strange one and no mistake, that Gregory. He had never been a biddable child like Michael and his sister, God rest their souls. How life had changed for Efim since he had first come eastward to this hard, windswept part of Siberia where even to survive the long winters took much courage and determination. He had built himself a pretty little house near a high waterfall and worked hard to make his farm prosper and his young wife happy.

And life had been contented enough, in the old days. Michael was born, and then the second son, Gregory. Michael had been docile enough, but Gregory resented discipline, preferring to fish or swim rather than pore over school books. But they were strong and sturdy sons, and life had prospered for them all until Efim's wife had died suddenly. Gregory was twelve then. And soon—too soon—afterwards, Michael had been snatched from them. Efim's rheumy old eyes watered as he remembered.

He had been hard at work mucking out the stable when

15

someone had called his name. He had come out, blinking in the sunlight and shielding his eyes with his hand. A stranger, a peasant, was supporting Gregory and Michael on either arm, and both of them were dripping pools of water on to the sunbaked cobblestones.

"These your lads?" the peasant had demanded.

"Aye. What's happened to them?" Efim had hurried forward and taken Michael's tottering figure from him.

"This one fell in the river and the other one," he nodded, indicating Gregory, "dived in after him. Lucky I was passing, 'cause the current's strong there and he was having a job keeping them both up. Reckon there's no harm done though, beyond a thorough soaking."

But the kindly peasant had proved wrong. Next day Michael ran a fever, and then became delirious. By nightfall he was dead—of a cracked skull, the doctor had said. He must have hit his head on a rock when he fell.

Gregory had become more withdrawn for a time after his brother's death. He, like his father, was shattered by the sudden gap left in their lives with both Mother and Michael gone. And then, as if Fate had not been cruel enough already, Gregory had rushed home one bright midday to disclose that his sister, too, had fallen victim to the Tura river. She had fallen in while washing their clothes, and was swept away and drowned. The shadow that fell over that summer's day had never left Efim since.

He knew he was perhaps at fault for the chasm that grew between himself and Gregory. He had been so enveloped in gloom and despair that he had had no time to communicate with his son. And the vodka had helped to blot out much of his misery, so that when he saw Gregory it was through an alcoholic haze and he could not remember whether they spoke to each other or not.

16

It was sufficient that when clarity returned he did not know his son, nor Gregory him. They were each alone, and could not turn to each other. Not that Gregory seemed to have need for anyone; he seemed self-sufficient and confident despite his youth. Even the village folk recognised it and respected him as they had once done Efim, though the lad was barely in his teens.

Efim glanced across the yard to where the derelict stable stood. It was in that doorway that he had learnt of Michael's death. The stable was long since disused except to harbour the chickens, for drinking had robbed Efim of the ability to work and misery had robbed him of the will. The horses were long since gone. The farm was no more than a cottage and a cluster of decaying outbuildings, and Efim tended no more than was necessary to eke out a bare existence. What was the point, with only Gregory left of all his family, and he would no doubt leave the village soon to make his own way in the world, for it was obvious Pokrovskoe would soon be too small for his abilities.

Despite the gulf between them, Efim could not resist a twinge of pride at the thought of him. Gregory had more to him than mere peasant ambition to own a farm. True enough, he had the normal young man's desires that set the old gossips' tongues clacking and complaints about his rapaciousness flowed freely. But what else could they expect of a young, lively, well-built fellow? Efim chuckled. He remembered his own youthful exploits had not been so different. But he had never had Gregory's strange, almost uncanny perception. It must be something he had inherited from his mother's side, for even from early childhood he had been impossible to deceive.

There was the incident of the goose, for instance. Gregory had been only four or five then, and passionately attached to

17

the squawking creature which followed him everywhere. So when the time had come to kill the goose, Efim had taken pains not to let Gregory know. He had sharpened his knife painstakingly in the kitchen while the child was out at play, but suddenly Gregory had burst into the kitchen, eyes sparkling with the excitement of the game. His gaze had become suddenly sober on seeing Efim, who was standing with the knife well hidden behind him.

"What are you doing with a knife behind your back, Papa?" the child had asked.

Efim was startled. Not only was the knife out of the child's view but it was covered by a kitchen cloth.

"What knife?" Efim had parried.

"The knife behind you—under the cloth."

"Can you see it?"

"Of course." Gregory had then come forward and reached behind him. Efim was too amazed to restrain him. The boy looked at him reproachfully, as he unwrapped the knife. "You weren't going to kill my goose, were you, Papa?"

"No, of course not." And he had not. It was another goose which lay on the platter at supper that night.

That had been the first time. After that there had been many occasions when Gregory had shown this phenomenal ability to see through things. A stolen loaf of bread wrapped in a boy's coat at school and secreted at the bottom of his desk, a mislaid wedding ring in a bale of hay, and then the strange business of the horse.

It was very odd, that evening the men had come to Efim's house, as head man of the village, to discuss the disappearance of a horse from a peasant's barn. The men had sat around, discussing earnestly how to trace the thief, completely ignoring the child who lay in the corner of the room on a sofa. Mother had brought Gregory, then about eight years of age,

18

from his bed to the living-room where she could keep an eye on him, for he had been running a high temperature all day and still looked flushed and excitable.

No one had been angrier or more bent on revenge against the thief than Bornikov, one of the richer peasants of the village. Mutilation, he averred, would be no more than the culprit deserved if and when they caught him.

The boy in the corner moaned. Efim turned to see if all was well. Gregory sat up slowly, his eyes shining with the heat of the fever, and pointed a finger at Bornikov.

"That man is the thief," his small voice said, high and clear, and then he sank back on the cushion.

Bornikov leapt to his feet. "How dare you!" he shouted. "Efim—will you let your child slander me so? I demand that you chastise him for his impudence directly!"

Efim cleared his throat apologetically. "Pay no heed to the boy, my friend, for he is ill and delirious with a fever. He does not know what he is saying, I assure you. Sit yourself down again and let us discuss how best we may catch the real thief."

Efim called out to his wife to fetch wine for his guests, and Bornikov grunted and sat down. But the seed of suspicion had been sown. Gregory had proved right so often before. So Efim had been gratified when two of the villagers, before bidding him goodnight, had confidentially declared their intention of following Bornikov. And more than gratified when he learnt later that they had crept behind him in the darkness and watched him take the stolen horse from his barn to set it free in the fields. But he had not avoided justice. The outraged villagers had given him a thorough beating before returning the horse to its owner.

Efim had been content. Once again Gregory's remarkable perception had been proved correct. Now even the local folk recognised his uncanny powers of second sight, and his reputation as a seer was born.

No wonder Efim was proud of his son who possessed such strange, mystical ability that was beyond the understanding of simple peasants like himself. And he worked hard as a wagoner for a contractor in Tobolsk, so undoubtedly he would soon feel the need to spread his young wings and fly further afield. The world would some day come to hear of the powers of young Gregory Efimovitch.

The sun had gone down now and the yard was growing chilly. Efim stood up, stretched his cramped limbs, and carried his chair indoors. Perhaps he had better set about preparing a meal against Gregory's eventual return. He fetched a large bowl of soup from the cupboard to heat, but the fire had died out. Efim shrugged and put the bowl away, taking out a loaf instead. He cut himself a large hunk of bread and some cheese. It really did not seem worth while re-lighting the stove to heat soup for only two of them.

It was fully dark by the time Gregory came home. Efim could hear him whistling as he stabled the horse and clattered across the yard to the cottage. He looked about him and sniffed.

"What's for supper, Father?"

Efim grunted and pushed the bread and cheese across the table. Gregory sighed and sat down and began cutting. Never complained, did Gregory, thought his father. He was a like-able, easy-going fellow. No wonder the village lasses eyed him appreciatively. Not specially handsome, perhaps, but an impressive figure with his wide grey eyes and sturdy broad shoulders. Was it a wench that had kept him out late tonight?

"Where have you been till now, lad? Did you have to stay late in Tobolsk?"

Gregory did not answer for a moment, his mouth working

busily as he chewed. He looked up, and Efim saw the black pupils of his eyes contract to a pinpoint as their gaze met. The surrounding blue-grey iris seemed to enlarge so swiftly as almost to engulf the pupil, and Efim was lost in wonder. He quite forgot what it was he wanted to ask Gregory.

The youth then went on eating in silence, save for the champing of his teeth on the crusty bread. Efim pushed back his chair and rose wearily. It was becoming cold in the little room with its flagstoned floor and ill-fitting windows now the fire was out. He had the choice either of sitting with his fur-lined coat about him or going to bed to keep warm.

Bed, that was the best place. Efim paused before the ikon of the Virgin Mary on the mantelshelf and felt a twinge of conscience. He crossed himself and muttered a swift prayer. In the old days it would not have been such a sketchy apology of a prayer, he mused. Then he would have gathered his family about him and read them a chapter from the Lives of the Saints, and they would all have knelt and prayed together. But that was in the old days, a symbol of what was gone and could never be retrieved.

At the doorway he looked back at his son, the boy's face clearly illuminated by the lamp on the table. The blue-grey eyes were watching him keenly, and Efim thought he could detect a hint of mockery in their gleam. Was his son, with his aura of uncanny perception, truly mocking him for his show of piety? Efim felt uneasy. Life was changing too fast for his slow old brain to keep up with it, and this strange son of his was the most perplexing part of it.

"I'm for bed, son. Are you coming?" he asked gruffly. If one could not put into words the real problems that pressed one, the next best thing was to talk of everyday matters.

"Soon. I may go out again yet." Gregory's reply was simple but uncommunicative. He made no attempt to disclose where or why he was going. Efim accepted his answer with resignation. Then he remembered his earlier question.

"What kept you tonight, son? Did you have to work late?"

This time Gregory did not look up and fix him with his odd, penetrating gaze. He tossed off a tankard of wine and then set the tankard down on the table with a thud. "No, I was not working late. I merely stopped on the way home to bring a little warmth and vitality into a poor creature's barren existence. You often taught us that that was an act of piety, Father."

Efim nodded. He had no idea what the boy meant, but he could not argue. It would seem the long hours of preaching religious principles to his children had had some effect after all. Or was his son still mocking him? He could not see the look in Gregory's eyes in order to determine, but true to his policy of leaving well alone, Efim let the matter be. He bade his son good night and mounted the stairs stiffly.

Shortly afterwards he heard the cottage door close and Gregory's footsteps cross the cobbled yard, but he fell asleep too early to hear what time the boy came home again.

THREE

FOR days Tanya loitered about in the places she felt she was most likely to encounter Gregory Efimovitch, but she was unlucky. Not once did she catch a glimpse of his broad frame, neither in the village square, nor in the river meadows nor even about the yard of his farm.

He must be away on one of his longer trips with the wagon, she concluded, carrying goods to some far-off place which was no more than a name to her. Even the village girls did not speak of him, elbowing each other out of the way at the pump in order to get their business done quickly and return home, for autumn chill was beginning to creep over Pokrovskoe and soon the bleak winter would come.

It was on the riverbank one morning as the women were washing clothes, their roughened fingertips showing blue against the cloth, that Tanya summoned up courage to ask about him as she watched. Katya's eyes snapped angrily as she scoured.

"Gregory? He hasn't been around for ages. Gone to carry a novice to the monastery at Verkhoture, I heard, but that was weeks ago and he's not back yet."

"Is that far, to Verkhoture?"

"Best part of a hundred miles. Why, you're not thinking of following him, are you?" Katya's expression was openly sneering. "I shouldn't, if I were you. Those who follow that Rasputin only come to grief. I'm glad I kept clear of him."

Tanya refrained from commenting that Gregory had obviously never looked at Katya with favour anyway, so the chance had never arisen. She was wondering what Katya's words meant, but feared the older girl's venomous tongue too much to ask. Katya's mouth was working furiously as her hands rubbed the clothes on the rocks.

"Did you hear Sasha was ill?" Katya said at last. Tanya shook her head. "Well, she is, and it's all his fault, the lecherous toad. Mind you, she was a fool and asked for it."

"What is wrong with Sasha?"

Katya glanced up curiously, then apparently decided to tell. "She found she was pregnant, that's what. And she went to someone she knew in the forest to give her a potion of some kind, tree bark or herbs or something, to help her get rid of it. But it didn't work, at least, not properly. She lost the baby, but she's near dying now, and no one can help her. It's all that Gregory Rasputin's fault, and if you're wise you'll avoid him like the plague, that's my advice."

She wrung the clothes out savagely and began to bundle up the washing to take home. Tanya walked away disconsolately. So Gregory was no longer the object of veneration amongst the local girls, she thought sadly. Or perhaps it was only Sasha who had reason to hate him now, and Katya since he had scorned her. Maybe the other big girls hoped for their chance still when he returned.

And so it seemed. Other village lads ogled the girls in the market place and made tentative passes at them, but Tanya noticed how the girls repulsed them and tittered amongst themselves, saying they would prefer to wait till the dashing Rasputin's return. So Tanya too was content to wait and hope. And as the weeks turned into months, and the winter snows came to lie over Pokrovskoe like an icy blanket, Gregory still did not return.

Tanya pushed her disappointment aside and put the waiting time to good use, with all the optimism and youthful hope that was in her. All the time he was gone she was still growing; with luck she could be a woman by the time he saw her again. Nightly she stood before the mirror and surveyed her figure wishfully. Surely she was not mistaken, and her shape was taking on a new and fuller roundness? She ran her hands down over firm young skin and prayed to the good Lord to send her breasts soon.

It was one day early in the New Year that Grandmother sent Tanya to Efim's cottage with a bowl of stew.

"Here, take this to Efim and bid him eat it quickly," she said abruptly as she placed the dish in a basket and packed it round with cloths to keep it warm. "Waste no time on the way or it will freeze," she admonished Tanya at the doorway, watching her go. She was a kind woman, thought Tanya. Despite the curtness of her tone, she felt truly sorry for the lonely old man who would not trouble to cook for himself. And though she despised his son, Grandmother still remembered Efim with warmth and respect as the man he used to be.

Efim came towards her in the yard, his bent figure huddled against the cold wind. In his hand he carried a pail of grain. Tanya gave him the basket and Grandmother's message, and he grunted surly thanks.

"Here, you take it and I'll feed the chickens for you," Tanya offered, taking the pail from him.

He nodded. "In the barn," he said, and went indoors. Tanya went into the barn. Its warm, dark atmosphere was a welcome change from the bitter chill outside. The chickens ran noisily about her, grabbing the grain eagerly and looking up expectantly for more. At last, the pail empty, Tanya put it down.

Above her head she could see the dim darkness of the hayloft running along one wall of the barn, and the wooden stepladder leading up to it. How often had Gregory lain up in that loft with one of the girls, she wondered. Curiosity to see the place where he had been often came over her. She climbed the ladder and stepped into the softly crackling warmth of the hay.

There was no hurry to return home. She would lie here a while and muse, imagining Gregory lying here too and wondering what his actions and thoughts had been. It was warm and comfortable here, and the foetid, animal smell of the place was bemusing to the senses. How long she lay there or whether she drowsed off she did not know, but suddenly she was aroused by the sound of footsteps below. She sat up quickly and rolled over to peer over the edge of the loft.

Her whole being stiffened with surprise and excitement. The tall broad figure in belted smock and boots silhouetted in the doorway was undoubtedly Gregory's. He was leading in a horse. She must indeed have been asleep not to hear the wagon cross the cobbled yard.

She shrank back in the shadows so as not to be seen. Much as she longed for and dreamt of being alone with him, she was shy at the thought of being discovered lurking thus in his hayloft. Efim could not have been expecting him home today, or surely he would have mentioned it.

She peeped gingerly over the edge. Gregory was whistling softly as he tethered the horse and gave it feed to eat. Then from outside a voice hailed him loudly. Gregory went to the door.

"Boris! How are you, my friend?"

He stepped back into the barn and Boris came in. He clapped Gregory heartily on the shoulder.

"We thought we had seen the last of you in Pokrovskoe, Rasputin. What happened, then? Did they take you in too as a novice at the monastery?"

Gregory's smile of welcome faded and he became serious.

26

"Not quite, though it is true I have spent all these last four months in Verkhoture. It is a fascinating place, Boris. You would not believe half of what I have seen."

"In a monastery? Come now, my friend, you'll be telling me they have parties and wenches next, else what could you find of interest in a prison like that?" Boris's voice was full of high good humour. Tanya crouched lower and prayed they would not discover her.

Gregory signalled Boris to sit down and he knelt eagerly beside him. "It is not a prison, Boris. It is more like a lovely old farmhouse set on a hilltop with the village and the river below. And apart from the monks who live there, several members of heretical sects are detained there and they are the most interesting of all."

"Heretics? Of what kind?" Boris asked.

"Oh, you know, sects like the Khlysty and the Skoptzy."

"I have heard of them, but I know little about them," Boris admitted slowly.

"No more did I, until now," Gregory said, and Tanya could hear the excitement in his voice. "But I came to learn a lot about the Khlysty. They believe in reaching God through atoning for sin."

"Well, of course. The Church teaches us that."

"But in order to atone, you have to sin first, don't you? So they do, often and regularly."

Boris contemplated the thought for a moment before questioning Gregory. "How?"

"Through carnal sin. They have secret sex orgies, very discreetly, you understand, every Saturday night. They dress up in white linen gowns, both the men and the women, and they meet in a clearing in the woods by candlelight. Then they sing hymns and chant and dance until they grow wild with excitement."

27

"And then?" Tanya could hear the eager curiosity in Boris's voice now.

"They strip off their clothes and the leader lashes them with a whip, and when they are absolutely mad with frenzy every man takes the nearest woman, whoever she is, and whether she's related to him or not."

"A brother and a sister?" Boris's voice was low with wonder.

"Or even father and daughter."

"And this is religion?"

"As I said, Boris, they believe in sin first and then atonement. What could be more logical?" Gregory's voice explained patiently.

"Did you take part in these orgies too, Gregory?"

Gregory shook his head. "But whether one agrees with their way of thinking or not, one cannot help but admire their fervour and vitality. Their beliefs are so much more alive and passionate than the orthodox church."

Tanya lay wide-eyed in the hay, staring into the darkness of the roof above her. She could understand but little of what he had been saying, but it was apparent that this strange heretical religion had inspired great admiration in Gregory.

"And I met an interesting old man while I was there too," Gregory went on. "A hermit he was, lived in a hut at the edge of the woods. Most folk believed him crazy, old Makary, but pilgrims came to ask his blessing, and I liked him too. He suggested I learn to write, for he felt I had a great future ahead of me. He bade me prepare for it now."

Boris was silent. Like Tanya, he too could barely understand Gregory, whose mind seemed to soar above the level of the village folk. Tanya heard him make for the door.

"So I shall prepare," Gregory said quietly. "I do not feel I shall spend my life in Pokrovskoe. It is too narrow for me, too stagnant. I need life and activity, where there is room for imagination and ambition."

Boris grunted. "Time I went home," he said gruffly. "Glad to see you back, Gregory."

Tanya heard his footsteps clatter away across the yard, and lay motionless until Gregory should leave too. The barn was silent now save for the muted chatter of the chickens. Minutes passed, and still she had not heard Gregory go. Then suddenly she stiffened with fear. She felt as though a ray of light was shining upon her, showing up her presence to the world.

"Come out, girl." Gregory's voice was low but vibrant with command. Tanya rolled to her knees and then stood up.

"Come down here."

She clambered down the stepladder clumsily, her long skirt tangling between her feet. At last she stood before him, penitent and ashamed. How could he possibly have seen her, well hidden in the darkness behind the hay? Unless the village folk's talk of him having second sight was true. Tanya shivered.

He did not speak. At length she found the courage to look up at him. His head was a clear foot above her own, and his pale grey eyes were fixed on her unblinkingly. The power of the stare frightened her, and Tanya's lip began to tremble.

"Have no fear, child, I shall not harm you," he said in a low voice. "I was simply curious as to why a child should lie and listen unseen in the loft. Why were you there?"

"I wanted to see you." Tanya's tone was timid, but his gaze remained firm and fierce.

"Why?"

Tanya tossed her head, conscious of her small, unvoluptuous appearance, but refusing to be browbeaten by this awe-inspiring youth whom all the girls sought. "Because I wanted you to seduce me," she said proudly, but inside she was quaking.

Gregory's eyes widened in surprise, then the black pupils shrank rapidly till they almost disappeared.

"But I don't any more!" Tanya cried suddenly. "I did, but I don't now!" And it was true. Maybe she had surrendered her one and only chance of achieving the status of womanhood and respect, but she did not want him to touch her. His clothes were ragged, his long brown hair straggling in greasy locks over his shoulders, his chin showed a grey stubble—and he smelt, abominably, of sweat and filth. In fact, there was nothing personable about him at all, if one excluded his eyes. They were his one attractive feature, clear and alive and strong.

"I see." He strode to the doorway, and then turned. "You are Tanya, are you not, from the cottage down near the river?"

"Yes."

"How old are you?"

"Twelve."

He rubbed the stubbled chin and looked thoughtful. "Then go home, Tanya. And maybe in a year or two you will come to me again, and that time maybe I will accommodate you."

Tanya raised her eyes doubtfully. "You think me too young?" she ventured. "Or too plain?"

He turned his back on her, so she could not see his expression as he answered.

"You will be beautiful soon, Tanya, and I shall remember you when I gather together my band of sister disciples." His voice was distant and dreamy. Suddenly he turned and smacked Tanya soundly on the bottom. "But for now—go home, child. You are too flat-chested for me yet."

She heard his laughter behind her as she ran across the

snow-flaked yard into the dusk. Despite the ice-cold wind whipping into her frozen face, her cheeks were scalded by tears of humiliation. Grandmother would scold her too when she arrived home without the basket and the soup bowl.

FOUR

GREGORY lay wide awake in his truckle bed and listened to the snores that emanated from the high old conjugal bed where Efim lay. Poor Father! He was a desperately lonely man, as Gregory had seen by the delight with which the old fellow had welcomed his profligate son home from Verkhoture some weeks ago.

Gregory felt pity for the old man, but mildly angry too that he made no effort to make something positive out of his life. He was kindly and loyal—as he had shown when the police came last week, sent by Gregory's employer in Tobolsk.

"A horse is missing, and your son must account for it," they had said, and even when the police had searched Gregory and found the twenty-one roubles in his pocket, Efim had refused to believe his son a thief. Gregory had explained how the horse had broken away from the tree where he had tethered it, and in the darkness it had fallen into the river which was swollen with melting snows. He could only surmise that the horse had drowned.

"And the money?" they had demanded. "Where would a peasant acquire twenty-one roubles?"

"A gift from the monks at Verkhoture when I left." They had been reluctant to accept his story, all except Efim, but in the end they had had to release him. Efim had gripped his hand tightly as the police left and never mentioned the incident again, though Gregory had sensed that even he had found it hard to believe that the monks had taken such a liking to him as to be thus generous. But it was true, they had.

Religious people seemed to be able to come by money easily, it seemed. It would be an easy life for anyone who could subject himself to the deprivations of the flesh that it would entail—a hair shirt, nourishing but sparse food, and no girls. Unless, of course, one turned religion to one's own ends like the Khlysty did, involving orgies as a means to salvation. That was clever—and logical too, if one considered it.

But he had enjoyed the monks' company, nonetheless; not for their religious principles, but for their intelligence and friendliness, their lack of stubborn prejudice and narrow thinking that marked the ordinary Russian peasant. Gregory's mind had been freed to soar, to find self-expression with them as it had never been able to amongst his own stupid and brutal folk.

One day he must leave Pokrovskoe for ever, he knew it now. The time was not yet ripe, but it must come. The village was too circumscribed to contain his potentiality. And it was all Verkhoture's doing, this revelation of the breadth of the world outside.

Still, there were pleasant things to occupy him in the meantime. Four months of self-denial made him eager for the village girls again, and although they had been slow to respond at first, they were beginning to yield shyly again now. It was some time before he heard of Sasha's illness which was the cause of their reluctance, but now she was apparently recovered and well again.

Then there was the festivity at the Aballakask convent to look forward to next week. Heaven alone knew which saint's festival they were celebrating, but it was of little account. They would be singing and dancing and merrymaking, and, like all peasants, he enjoyed the fun of a festival. Wrapping the pleasant prospect about him like another blanket, Gregory drifted off to sleep.

When the night of the festival arrived, Efim decided not to go with Gregory.

"It is too far for my old legs to walk in this cold weather," he said gloomily. "I shall stay by the fire, but you go with Boris."

But Boris could not go either, for his father had need of him in his forge. So Gregory set out for Aballakask alone, feeling his insides mounting with excitement as he crossed the snow-covered fields with long, deliberate strides. Long before he reached the convent he could hear the bells echoing out across the snow, and the tinkle of sleigh bells as the faithful converged at the convent.

It was warm in the chapel with so many fur-wrapped bodies pressed closely together, and with the lusty singing and the odour of incense Gregory felt his heart warming with exhilaration and love of his fellow beings. It was the kind of love that needed expression.

Then they danced in the old hall, and Gregory's senses reeled with the proximity of warm bodies sweating in their exertion. In the throng he found occasion easily to press firm young maidens to him, and the yearning to make up for lost time in Verkhoture, to seize a wench and drag her out to a barn, almost made him breathless. It was enough to make one feel sick, this urgent desire to express his joy and love of mankind. Although he had not drunk a drop yet this evening, his head reeled with pure animal intoxication.

In the midst of the dance he suddenly stopped. A flaxen-haired maid with the purest, sweetest expression he had ever seen was smiling at him, and Gregory's heart lurched in anticipation. This was the one—this, undoubtedly, was the wench who should give him the means to express his joy.

Easy, man, easy, he exhorted himself. She looked a better class of girl than the local wenches and would not welcome a brash, impudent approach. He surveyed her admiringly from a distance. How smoothly she moved, how graceful and delicate in every way! Her smooth gold hair was piled on top of her head in neat plaits, and her cheeks were rounded and flushed with exertion. Her blue eyes sparkled and her figure was slim and shapely, far removed from the buxom generosity of Sasha and the local girls. She was entrancing. Before long he must find the occasion to contrive a meeting in a private place.

He found himself next to her at the long table where refreshing drinks were being served. She looked bewildered in the crush of people, so Gregory offered to fetch a drink for her. She smiled gratefully.

"What is your name?" he asked as they sat in a corner. Usually he did not waste time on exchanging names, but this girl was different.

"Praskovie Dubrovine." Her answer was shy and gentle. What an angel she was!

She was alone at the festival, he discovered to his delight. Trying not to appear too wildly eager, he offered to accompany her safely home, and could have roared aloud with delight when she agreed. Her village was some miles from Pokrovskoe, but the walk in the snow did not deter him. To find satisfaction with such a creature was worth a few miles' walk.

But Praskovie apparently had other ideas. Though Gregory induced her to shelter under a hedge when it suddenly began to snow more heavily, she would not agree to his suggestion that they cuddle closely together for warmth, and removed his prying fingers firmly. Again when he drew her into a barn on the outskirts of her village, she shook her head firmly.

"But why not?" said Gregory in his most wheedling tones. "You like me, don't you?"

"Yes, but please leave me alone."

He kissed her often, tenderly and passionately, but although she responded gently, she still kept hold of his hands when they roamed. At last, worn out from this unaccustomed restraint, Gregory resorted to his usual tactics and pressed her down hard in the hay. The blue eyes glared at him angrily.

"Gregory, stop it this minute. I am no village whore and I won't have you treat me as one."

He sat back and looked at her meaningfully, with the concentrated look that usually hypnotised his girls into instant submission. But to no avail. Praskovie sat up, buttoned her blouse and rose to go. Gregory was so surprised at his failure that he rose and accompanied her to her door.

"Shall I see you again?" he asked.

"If you wish."

"I shall call for you tomorrow evening then."

She nodded and went in. As Gregory plodded homeward through the snow he could only marvel at himself. He, Gregory Efimovitch, otherwise known as Rasputin, the rake, had been known to take two or even three girls in an evening before his lust was satisfied, and yet tonight, with his insides burning him as fiercely as this, he had let a gentle creature turn him down. What was wrong with him? His lust burned as fiercely as ever—yet he wanted no other girl to assuage it, only this pale-haired, sloe-eyed maiden who was as puritanical as she could be.

He went to his cold bed with his ardour still unsatisfied, and longed for the following evening to come. But still Praskovie did not relent. Nor on the next occasion. No matter how he importuned her, whether he leapt to the attack like a famished beast or cajoled her with pleading tones, Praskovie remained quietly firm and resolute.

"No, Gregory, I am sorry but the answer is no." And so it

went on for weeks. Gregory became obsessed with the girl who was so different from all others he had known, and so different from himself too. He was pure peasant—rough, dirty and uncouth—while she was gentle and refined. He was lustful and she was pure. He was ambitious, abrupt and demanding, but she was contented, polite and full of admiration for him.

The winter snows melted from the village and from the fields beyond, but Praskovie remained as frozen as the ice had been. Gregory could bear the yearning inside him no longer.

"I am going to get married," he told a startled Efim one spring evening.

Efim, who was gutting a chicken, let the knife fall from his hand. He looked up wide-eyed at his son.

"Married? You? You're too young!"

"I am nineteen, and that is old enough. And you have often said we need a woman about the place."

Efim nodded. "True enough. Who is she?"

"Her name is Praskovie Dubrovine. You do not know her, but you will like her, Father. She will make me a fine wife and bear me fine sons to work on the farm."

That argument was sufficient for Efim, as Gregory well knew. All he had to do now was to ask Praskovie to marry him.

She listened intently while he told her of his plans to give up working as a wagoner and to try to rebuild his father's farm instead. She nodded from time to time but made no comment. At length he came to the point.

"Will you marry me, Praskovie?"

"Yes."

It was as simple as that. She did not ask any questions or ask his reason, and as she was already twenty-two, four years older than he, she did not need to say that he must wait until she had asked her parents. The difference in their ages

37

bothered Gregory not in the least. She was the kind of woman he wanted—desirable, straightforward and honest and completely docile. And so the matter was settled.

But still Praskovie would not anticipate the wedding date. She insisted on remaining untouched until they were properly bound in holy wedlock. Gregory complied. After all, it would be the last thing she would ever be able to dictate. After marriage she would have to obey him in everything.

On the day of his wedding, Gregory took special pains over his toilet. For once he washed, not just a splash at the pump but a thorough wash. And he put on a clean tunic and brushed his serge breeches and scraped the years of accumulated mud off his boots. After a search he unearthed a comb and cursed furiously as he tried to untangle his long locks, but at last he was ready. Efim beamed at him proudly.

Praskovie looked angelic as she knelt beside him at the altar while the priest made his incantations, and Gregory felt inordinately proud as he led her on his arm out of the church into the pale spring sunlight. He could see the lecherous looks on the village lads' faces and knew they envied him his bridegroom's task. One wistful little face caught his eye among the throng of merrymaking villagers—it was the little wench from down by the river, Tanya. Her large eyes were watching him with a forlorn, woe-begotten expression. He smiled at her contentedly, and saw her turn and run away into the crowd.

That night, after the feasting and drinking had ended, he held Praskovie close in his arms in the high old bed his father had vacated in deference to the young couple. Efim was no doubt snoring off the effects of the wine in a far corner of the farmhouse. Gregory felt content. Praskovie was a pliant, if not yet passionate, partner, but she was all he had anticipated for so long.

"Are you happy, Praskovie?"

"Yes."

She snuggled down in the hollow of his arm and went to sleep. What a nice, uncomplicated girl she was!

Spring came slowly to the village and the crops sprouted and Efim whistled happily as he set to mending the long-broken fences. Praskovie moved placidly about the kitchen and brought a new warmth to the long-neglected household. For a time Gregory's world was sunlit and the birds sang. He had his hands full with the farm to re-stock and rebuild, and a young wife to adjust to. Not that Praskovie demanded any adjustment; she was content for Gregory and his father to act as they had always done, and she fitted in unobtrusively, providing fresh linen and hot meals with a smile.

Then, without anyone noticing how it came about, she seemed suddenly to be withdrawn and lost in a private world. Her eyes were dreamy and far-away when Gregory called her to fetch more wine, and he had to shout again. He wondered irritably what ailed the girl, and resolved to speak to her about it when they were alone in the privacy of their bedroom. There was no time for day-dreaming on a busy farm.

But he was taken aback at Praskovie's gentle reply to his reproach.

"Forgive me, Gregory. I did not mean to neglect you, and shall take care not to again. You see, we are to have a child."

FIVE

Hot summer days cooled into autumn and now the first icy fingers of winter were beginning to be felt in Kokrovskoe. Gregory began to grow restless. His first sensation of pride and wonder and elation at becoming a father had been wonderful, and he could not resist the joyous urge to burst into song at his work whenever he thought about it. Efim too had been dourly satisfied. The family line was to continue and the farm he had laboured long to establish would be secure.

But that was months ago. Praskovie still moved happily though now rather cumbersomely about the kitchen, but she seemed more remote than ever. When she lay next to Gregory in the high soft bed at night she would lie wide-eyed and unsleeping, but never speaking unless his hands reached out for her.

"No, not now, Gregory. Think of the child."

Her whole mind and being seemed to be absorbed with the coming child, and Gregory began to grow impatient and irritable. But however he snapped at Praskovie, she did not seem to notice or to mind, and continued her daily chores contentedly.

If only the child were born, Gregory thought, then all could return to normal. Who could blame him if his eyes lingered overlong on a buxom village wench while Praskovie remained so remote and unloving? And the village girls were willing enough too, he knew from experience, so where would be the harm in satisfying their demands at the same time as his own?

It was not long before the opportunity presented itself,

almost as though it had been pre-destined. He was walking home over the fields one late afternoon when a sudden shower of hailstones drove him to find shelter. A near-by barn beckoned invitingly. Gregory dashed inside.

A girl sat on a mound of hay, clutching a basket of eggs. Her dark eyes glistened at the sight of him and Gregory recognised the signal. He sat down beside her and reached for her blouse buttons in silence. She smiled and did not move till he pushed her down in the hay.

It was so easy. Girls seemed to like the look of him at first sight, and perhaps they recognised the driving, animal force in him. At any rate, they always complied readily, never asking for polite wooing first, and he would be a fool, he reasoned, not to take advantage of their willingness.

So he passed the dreary waiting time while Praskovie was so dreamy and preoccupied, in this pleasant manner, at first secretly and well away from home, but as time passed he grew more daring and even took advantage of his own barn, right under Praskovie's nose. If she knew, she never spoke of it to him. Once Boris relayed the story to him over the ale one night of how an outraged country woman had upbraided Praskovie for not keeping a stricter eye on her husband's activities.

"It seems he can lay half the wenches in the village and no one cares!" she stormed. Praskovie had shrugged calmly. "He has enough for us all," she replied gently. Gregory was very pleased. She was a good wife, sensible and efficient, and if she had the good sense to turn a blind eye to her husband's goings-on, it was because she knew full well he would never abandon her. He congratulated himself on his choice of such a sensible girl.

It was near Christmas when the child was born. Efim came

stumbling out to the fields where Gregory was searching for a lost sheep.

"Come, Gregory! Praskovie is near her time! The midwife is with her now!"

They had hastened home to find Praskovie lying pale and contented, the baby in her arms. Like a good sheep, she had dropped her burden quickly and without difficulty, Gregory thought proudly.

"I have borne you a son," Praskovie said gently, holding the child up to him.

A son! Pride glowed fiercely in Gregory's veins. He looked at the little red, puckered face and marvelled. Old Efim grunted contentedly into the little face and fell asleep.

Gregory Efimovitch celebrated his son's birth royally that night. With his cronies Petcherkine and Barnaby and Boris he drank a toast again and again to the little son's health and could scarcely remember rolling home to his bed. He had a hazy impression that some fair-haired wench at the inn had helped him round off his evening's celebrations, for the feel of her yielding soft flesh still vibrated in his fingertips, but he could not recall her name, if he ever knew it.

For the next few months life retained its even tenor. Gregory's pride in his son did not diminish, nor in his gentle young wife, but he did not forgo the pleasure the village girls had to offer. The nickname of Rasputin he had earned clung to him still.

Then one evening he sat drinking and laughing with Boris and Barnaby in the inn. Suddenly a white-faced Efim lurched in and stared about him. Gregory called to him.

"Come and have a drink with us, Father."

Efim clutched his arm. "Come home, Gregory. The boy is sick."

Gregory smiled. "Has he brought up his feed again, then?

I swear Praskovie's milk is too rich for him. She is a fertile cow, my wife, and will bear me many more such fine young bullocks. Do not fret yourself, Father."

But Efim's eyes were wide with fear. "It is not that kind of sickness, Gregory. He is pale and sweating and his eyes roll horribly. Praskovie bade me tell you to come instantly."

Gregory's heart lurched. No harm could come to such a healthy child, surely? He had survived nearly six months, past the danger time for new-born babies. But he could not resist the icy finger of fear that clutched his heart. He pushed his chair back.

"I am coming."

He left swiftly, without bidding his companions good night, and followed Efim's lumbering figure along the village street.

"He was not sick today. He was smiling at me this morning," he said defiantly to the old man.

Efim made no answer but hastened more quickly. It was Gregory who reached the door first, and he could hear the sound of Praskovie wailing inside.

She knelt over the cot, holding the baby's little body up to her breast. The child did not move. Gregory wrenched her away and heard her shriek as he bent to the child. It was too late. Not a breath stirred the little chest and the eyes were rolled upwards in their sockets. He was dead.

Gregory roared like a maddened bull and threw Praskovie's arms away from him. He lurched drunkenly out through the cottage door and ran, ran till his bursting lungs could draw no more breath, then he flung himself full length on the grass and wept. How long he roared and wept and cursed he did not know, nor did he care. What cruel injustice it was, to rob him of his first-born son, his pride and his manhood! He cursed God for this cruelty.

Hours later he lay, spent and exhausted, on the damp grass

43

and wiped his eyes with his dirty smock. By the time he reached home dawn was streaking the eastern sky and he found Praskovie sleeping in the chair, her hair straggling round her shoulders and her face tear-stained.

The child was buried, but Gregory could feel no more pain. His eyes burnt in their sockets and searched fruitlessly about him in an effort to understand what the boy's death meant. He could find no will to work and sat around the cottage all day, trying in vain to understand, and paid no heed to Praskovie's soothing words.

All he could see was that his life now was as futile as old Efim's had become, once he had been robbed of his family. Gregory could not bear the prospect of his life stretching before him in an endless, barren waste, simply marking time until death came. Oh, what was the point of life at all, once one was bereft of purpose? If he were to keep his reason, he must find some plausible explanation or he would shrivel and die. But with whom could he talk of his problem? Praskovie and Efim were well-meaning enough, but they were simple souls and it would be beyond their capabilities to understand his philosophical searching.

Makary—he was the man! The wise old hermit near Verkhoture—he would understand the dilemma and help him reason it out. Gregory made up his mind to seek the old man's help at once.

Praskovie did not question his journey, but packed up his clothes and food in silence. The village priest, Father Peter, did not encourage Gregory's proposed visit to the hermit, but Gregory suspected the priest believed him to be visiting Verkhoture once again only in order to join the Khlysty's orgiastic revels. Let him think what he wished. Gregory's need of Makary was too great to be hindered by such petty suspicions. The villagers sniggered amongst themselves and it came to Gregory's ears that they believed he had "got religion" after his baby's death, and was now no longer a rake but a "Godseeker". He ignored it all.

Makary welcomed him kindly to his little hut in the woods and murmured words of comfort, urging patience and resignation. Gregory knelt and prayed with him, but revelation did not come. Eventually Makary sent him home, still troubled and unable to find peace, and urged him to seek fulfilment in his work. Gregory ploughed his fields and prayed, but depression lay heavy on his soul.

Then one day the miracle happened. Gregory followed his plough in the spring sunshine, praying and brooding. Something made him look up, and there, in the sky above him, he saw the image of a woman, dressed in strange clothes, and recognised it instantly as the Virgin. He caught his breath. It was a sign from Heaven, but what did it signify? As he wondered, the image beckoned to him, then faded.

"You've been drinking," was Efim's laconic comment when his son rushed him with the news of his vision. Praskovie stared.

"I haven't touched a drop," Gregory protested.

"It could indeed be a sign," Praskovie murmured. "But what does it mean?"

"Nonsense!" growled Efim. "You'd be better occupied getting the ploughing finished in time for sowing."

Gregory was bewildered. He had Praskovie's support, if not Efim's, but he needed guidance as to the meaning of his vision. He decided to consult Makary again. Praskovie waved him off, but Efim growled.

"He has turned a pilgrim out of laziness, that one."

This time Makary listened in astonishment and pondered deeply. At length he pronounced his verdict.

"It is indeed a heavenly sign, my son. God has chosen you

45

for a great achievement. In order to strengthen your spiritual power you should go to Mount Athos."

Mount Athos! Gregory gasped. Mount Athos was in Greece, two thousand miles away! But if God wanted him to travel thus far, He must indeed have singled Gregory out for a great purpose. His soul grasped at the idea and soared. Whatever it was he was to be called upon to do, he would perform it well, with all the strength and single-mindedness he could muster.

SIX

It was all settled. Gregory was almost ready to depart on his mammoth journey, and his friend Petcherkine had agreed to accompany him. At last Gregory began to feel a measure of contentment. Now he would discover his life's purpose.

He was nearing his cottage the night before his departure when a shadowy figure emerged from the bushes at the roadside. It was a girl. Gregory peered at her in the dusk, and recognised the little maid, Tanya.

"Gregory Efimovitch,' 'she said solemnly, "I hear you are to leave soon on a long pilgrimage."

"That is so. I leave tomorrow."

"I cannot bear to think of you so long alone. Will you let me come with you?" Her dark eyes gleamed hopefully.

Gregory laughed. "I already have a travelling companion, child. Petcherkine is to come with me. Now what use would I have for a little maid like you? Go home to your grandmother, and maybe when I return I shall tell you of my travels. Will that content you?"

The girl looked downcast, but nodded. "I did not know you had a companion. I shall wait for you. How long will you be gone?"

"Months—maybe years. But I shall return when I discover what I seek. Now hurry home before it is dark, Tanya."

The girl sped away into the gloom, and Gregory continued homeward. What a funny little thing she was, always dogging him and yet so reserved. In a year or two she would be an eye-catching wench for the village lads, he could see. He hugged Praskovie as she leaned over the table with his dish of stew.

"Will you miss me, wife?"

"Yes. But I shall be busy."

He knew what she meant. There were indications that she might be pregnant again, but the possibility did not enliven him. His projected pilgrimage was the one vast subject which filled his whole mind and being.

How long would it be before he saw his wife and father again, he wondered. It was 1891 now, and the years could have slipped by before he returned. And how changed would he be after his voyage of discovery? Would he return an enlightened man, or disillusioned and bereft of hope? He refused to consider the latter possibility. The journey would shed new light on problems which had long perplexed him, and it would be a new and wiser man who came back to Pokrovskoe, he felt convinced of it.

So next morning at first light he and Petcherkine set forth, both dressed in the long robes of pilgrims and carrying a pilgrim's staff. The journey was long and hard, but they found Siberian village folk were kindly disposed towards pilgrims and treated them with respect. By night they could always be sure of a bowl of soup when they knocked at cottage doors, and if not the luxury of a bed, at least a warm corner by the stove to sleep.

Peasants everywhere welcomed them with hospitality, and before four months had passed, Gregory and his friend reached their goal, the group of monasteries that clustered on Mount Athos. They were footsore and weary, but excited. Petcherkine was so elated that he became a novice without delay, but Gregory hesitated. In his heart he still doubted the orthodox church, for he remembered the exuberance of the banned sects like the Khlysty which seemed to carry more conviction. So he watched cautiously while Petcherkine took his initial vows and kept silent.

He did not care for the monks there, holy though they seemed. They had an air of cold asceticism which did not appeal to his hot nature in the least, and a secretive, clannish atmosphere enveloped them.

One night he returned to the cell he shared with a pale-faced and, as yet, beardless youth named Basil who seemed to spend hours on his knees in the cold cell imploring God's forgiveness. What sin he had committed that demanded endless penitence Gregory did not know, but as he entered the cell he stopped in astonishment.

An aged, grey-haired monk was leaning over Basil's naked, white figure, his cassock drawn up about his waist. At the sight of Gregory he dropped his cassock instantly, his face burning red with embarrassment, muttered a few words and fled. Basil leapt up, grabbed his hair shirt and pulled it on convulsively, murmuring confused words of explanation.

"No need to explain," Gregory snapped curtly, and strode out again. He felt sickened. He went straight in search of Petcherkine.

"I am leaving this place," he told him shortly. "There is nothing here but dirt and vermin."

He would not explain his meaning, and Petcherkine was puzzled. "But you wanted so much to come here. I cannot leave now I have taken my vows, so you must stay."

"I will not. There is nothing for me in Mount Athos."

"Then where will you go?"

Gregory pondered. "Having come so far south, I could go on to the Holy Land. It is less than a thousand miles from here. Yes, that is what I shall do. I shall leave next week."

And despite Petcherkine's protestations he left. Makary had been wrong about Mount Athos—he had achieved no enlightenment there, but it was instrumental in driving him on to the Holy Land. Perhaps he would find meaning and contentment there.

Syria and Jordan made a fantastically deep impression on his peasant soul. The sorrow of Golgotha affected him deeply, and he was glad Makary had persuaded him to learn to write. Having no companion to share his emotions, he poured forth his feelings on paper.

"How impressive is Golgotha! . . . When you look at the place where the Mother of God stood, tears come to your eyes and you see before you the whole scene. Oh, God! What a deed was wrought!"

The vision of the Virgin he had seen in the field at Pokrovskoe haunted him. She too had known the harrowing suffering of losing a son as he had done. She could understand his misery and bewilderment.

And on the homeward journey through Kazan he stopped to pray at the cathedral. He lowered his head in prayer, and as his eyes rose again he caught sight of a statue near the altar. He went closer to it. It was an image of the Virgin— and she was dressed in exactly the way he had seen her in his vision in the fields.

This was an omen, he was certain of it! It was a sign that he had been meant to undertake the pilgrimage to the Holy Land! Whatever the course was that heaven had pre-destined for him, he was following it.

Gregory turned his weary footsteps towards Siberia. He knew now that he was on the right path, and God would determine the rest. Thousands of miles now separated the old life from the new, and Gregory marched with determination towards Pokrovskoe.

More than two years had elapsed since he left. It was now late in 1893, but the village had not changed. As he walked along its main street he marvelled how time could pass and leave no mark on the place or its people. The little stone cottages seemed to have the same chickens and pigs littering their yards, and the peasants wore the same belted smocks and boots. A few heads looked a little greyer, but their owners looked at him curiously and did not smile.

Suddenly he felt a tug at his sleeve. He looked down at a pretty dark-haired girl with a full, rounded figure thrusting beneath her cotton blouse and a radiant smile on her face.

"Gregory Efimovitch! You are home at last! Welcome, welcome back to Pokrovskoe!"

He looked at her curiously, and it was some moments before he recognised her.

"Tanya! Is it really you?"

She laughed and threw back her head, her white teeth gleaming in the sunlight.

"I have waited, as I promised. And I hope you will honour your promise to tell me all you have seen and done on your travels, for I have waited a long time for this."

She cocked her head on one side and regarded him thoughtfully. How pretty she had grown! He had been right in his surmise that she would become a very attractive filly. She had the fresh, clean innocent air of youth and hope about her that cheered his saddened soul.

"What are you thinking, Tanya?"

"How you are changed, Gregory, but your eyes are the same. You are thinner and you have a beard. You look like a man now, not a youth."

He smiled. "Is that all?"

"No." She considered for a moment. "You are changed so much I wonder if people will know you. You were so full of life before, and now . . ."

"Now?"

51

"Now you are sadder and older."

"But you recognised me, Tanya."

She smiled pertly. "I would always know you, for you were my first love, Gregory, when I was a child. Now I am fifteen and grown up."

"And no longer your first and only love?"

She laughed and ran away, her skirts flying out behind her and the chickens scattering from her path. Gregory sighed and turned in at the gate of his own farm.

It looked exactly as it had done when he left. The yard was neat and freshly-laundered curtains hung at the windows. Efim and Praskovie had carried on as if nothing had ever happened, it seemed. He wondered idly if they would recognise him. It would be interesting to see.

Instead of walking in through the door, Gregory knocked. Praskovie answered, pushing a stray wisp of hair back into the neat plait that surmounted her forehead. She was flushed with exertion.

"Yes?" Her voice held a note of patient curiosity and her eyes searched his face without a flicker of recognition. Gregory looked down at the ground.

"I am selling materials, mistress, from St Petersburg," Gregory replied in gruff tones. "Would you like me to show you?" He indicated the pack on his back, but Praskovie's brow furrowed at the sound of his voice.

"Who are you?" she said tremulously, and her eyes sought his. Gregory looked up at her then, and could not help the gleam of amusement in his eyes. "I know your voice," she said in a whisper. "And those eyes. . . ."

Gregory caught her up in his arms and whirled her round the little room. "Yes, I am home, wife! Gregory Rasputin is home again!"

SEVEN

IN THE little village the news travelled fast that the wandering pilgrim was home, the rake who had gone to seek God. Curious villagers came knocking at the door to welcome him home and see what changes had been wrought in him.

He looked much the same, they found. He still had the filthy, unkempt appearance of his rakish days, his shirt tied carelessly about his waist with a knotted rope, baggy trousers, and sandals on his dirty feet. A long, matted beard was a new development, but it was so scanty that the outline of his jaw could still be discerned through it, and his hands still showed the farmyard grime and blackened nails they had always shown. The long, straight hair straggled either side of his face from a centre parting, and through the gap his grey eyes shone from the pale face.

Yes, his eyes had not changed, the peasants averred. They still had the strange, mesmerising effect when he stared solemnly at one. One was no longer aware of the high forehead and the broad, prominent nose and full mouth, for the eyes dominated all else. Set deep under bushy eyebrows, their pupils seemed to bore into one's very soul.

"Those eyes have seen the Holy Land, where our Lord suffered and died," the peasants murmured in awe, and crossed themselves fervently, for were they not in the presence of a starets, a holy man? There was now about him an impressiveness, an aura of sanctity. He was no longer the village Rasputin, the ne'er-do-well, but a man of God. Had he not always, from a child, had the gift of second sight? He

53

was a man to venerate, to respect, despite his youth, and they doffed their caps and knelt for his blessing before they left Praskovie to tidy up the cottage again after their frequent intrusions.

She did not seem to mind, Gregory noticed, that he was now sought after day and night, bringing disruption to the formerly smooth life on the farm. She was maternally satisfied, with a new little occupant in the cradle beside the big bed and her husband home from his travels.

The baby was a boy—Dimitri, she had named him in Gregory's absence. Gregory looked down at the child and felt a strangeness about him.

"Is he strong?" he asked.

Praskovie strugged. "He eats well and grows sturdier every day. But he has strange fits from time to time which frighten me, but they pass."

Efim grunted, but when Praskovie's back was turned he muttered to his son, "That child is a runt, a weakling if ever I saw one. You must beget more sons soon if they are to till the land."

His rheumy eyes flickered hopefully. "And you too will begin work again on the farm now you are home, will you not? It has been heavy work for an old man like me and we need your broad shoulders."

But Gregory made no answer. He simply fell to his knees before the ikon of the Virgin on the mantelshelf and began to pray, lengthily. At last Efim left him, still on his knees, and went to bed.

A loud knocking at the cottage door awoke the household far into the night. A peasant, cap in hand, clutched Gregory's nightshirt in supplication.

"It's my wife, Gregory Efimovitch. She is sick unto death,

I fear, and the priest is away in another village. Come to her, I beg you, and pray for her!"

Gregory dressed without answering and strode off into the night after the peasant's terrified figure. All night he knelt by the woman's beside, holding her thin, wasted hand and praying. In the morning she was sleeping peacefully, and Gregory returned home exhausted.

The woman recovered. The news of Gregory's seeming power to rescue her from death spread like wildfire about the village, and day after day he found himself being entreated to pray for this sick soul or lay his beneficent hands on that crippled one. The peasants' implicit faith in the starets' power wrought seeming miracles, and they showed their gratitude in kind. Every day Praskovie found a chicken or a new-baked loaf, a scarf or a pair of boots left on her doorstep, and sometimes even a kopek or two.

Never once nowadays was Gregory Rasputin to be seen drinking in the village inn, nor did he even so much as pass an admiring glance at a pretty wench, let alone try to undo her blouse. The image he had once projected of the lazy, lecherous rake was gone. Now he was the saintly man, given to good works and prayer.

Efim began to grow irritable. Gregory was making no effort to help in the work of the farm although he had been home for some time now. One day he tackled his son on the subject.

"When are you going to stop all this praying and start work? You have lazed about for long enough," he protested indignantly. He put down the heavy buckets of water he was carrying and stood, hands on hips, glaring at Gregory malevolently.

His son looked up from the book he was reading, a mild expression of surprise on his face. "I? I shall no longer work a farm, Father. I have decided instead to build an oratory in the courtyard, where the villagers may pray with me."

Efim exploded. "What are you, boy, a farmer or a monk? It seems to me you must make up your mind! An oratory in the yard, for heaven's sake! Are you out of your mind?"

Gregory smiled and made no answer. But when the villagers heard of his plan they rallied to his side instantly, and in weeks they had laid the stones for him, delighted to be able to help their own starets.

He spent hours on his knees in prayer in the oratory, and Efim fumed in silence. Only once did he break the silence to retort maliciously when they found Praskovie was to bear another child, "Ah, so you are not entirely the monk, it seems. You have taken no vow of celibacy."

Ignoring the jibe, Gregory went on praying. But it grew cold out of doors and he wanted to pray with the local folk, so he decided to hold prayer meetings in the farm itself. Efim disappeared from sight whenever the peasants turned up, but Praskovie watched admiringly from a corner seat. Not many women were blessed with a holy man for a husband as she was. But after a time she kept out of the room while the meetings were in progress for she could not understand all Gregory was saying, and in any case there were other domestic tasks waiting to be attended to. She knew the room was always crowded, mostly with women, so her vacant seat would soon be filled.

She was quite unprepared for the sudden attack that came upon her goodly husband. As she walked along the village main street one day she met Father Peter, the priest, coming out of the church.

"Good day," he said courteously enough, and fell in beside her. He had talked about Gregory and the feeling of the people for him, then asked her about the prayer meetings.

"What do they do, in these meetings?"

"Oh, I don't know. I don't go any more as I'm busy. Pray, I suppose. Gregory is always praying."

"Do men go, or women?"

"Both, I think, but mostly women."

"And you have no idea what they do?"

"No."

"I believe your husband was very impressed by the beliefs of the Khlysty, was he not, when he went to Verkhoture?"

Praskovie looked startled. "Khlysty? What is that? I have never heard of it."

"No? No matter."

He had asked then about Gregory's prayer over sickbeds and people's gratitude, but Praskovie in her innocence had suspected no evil intention on Father Peter's part. She told Gregory of the incident. His wide grey eyes narrowed into pinpoints as he listened.

"We shall hear more of this, I fear," was his only comment.

And indeed they did. Within weeks they discovered that Father Peter had denounced Gregory Rasputin to the Bishop of Tobolsk as a heretic, suggesting he was an active member of the Khlysty and holding orgiastic meetings. He had demanded an investigation into the prayer meetings, and the Bishop had agreed.

Praskovie was terrified, feeling herself the innocent cause of the investigation. Gregory soothed her fears as they sat at supper.

"It is no more than I expected, my dear. Father Peter is understandably jealous of my reputation, for it cannot be easy to find one's position of local holy man usurped by a younger man, a layman at that."

"But what will you do, Gregory?"

Efim snorted. "Take off the hair shirt and get back to the

plough, if he's any sense. Give up the charade of being a starets."

Praskovie was shocked. "But Gregory is not acting! You have seen for yourself what he has done. How could you suggest it?"

"And what else can he do, now he's accused like this? Do you want him to go to prison?"

Praskovia looked pleadingly at her husband. "What can we do, Gregory? Tell me what you want to do, and I shall agree, whatever it is."

"I shall leave here."

It was not what she had expected to hear. In the eight years of their marriage she had seen so little of her husband. Praskovie's eyes grew moist and she tried to prevent them filling with tears. "Leave me, and Dimitri—and the child who is to come?"

Gregory sighed and stood up from the table. "I do not wish to argue with Father Peter or the Church, for I am tired and they are strong. It would be better if I disappeared quietly— for a time at least—until the uproar has died down. But I shall come back, have no fear."

"Where will you go, husband?"

Gregory shrugged. "St Petersburg, perhaps. I have never seen life in the city, with all the grand folk and fine houses and carriages. Perhaps, if they are too preoccupied with worldly things, I can spread the gospel there."

"You are a fine man, Gregory," Praskovie murmured in admiration. Even in adversity he could find some way to bring positive good out of misfortune.

She packed his clothes into a bundle, sadly. Yet again she would have to face the birth of a child alone.

EIGHT

No ONE saw Gregory leave the village, with the exception of Tanya, who was sitting on a grass hillock clutching her knees and gazing into space when he passed. She leapt up at once at the sight of him carrying a bundle and stick, and came running.

"Are you leaving again, Gregory, so soon?"

"Yes, child. I must go, but I shall return."

"Make it soon, for all the village folk love and admire you, Gregory, and we shall miss you."

She was as graceful as a deer, the way she ran back along the street. She was the last sight of Pokrovskoe he carried in his memory during the next year or so, wandering as he did from door to door until he reached St Petersburg.

It was a long journey. As he walked, slanting spring sun gave way to brief summer and then winter's heavy snows, through which tall pines and occasional log huts protruded. Flat, wide rivers, sweeping forests and immense desolate marshes where a man could think in peace were replaced by busy little villages where men and women worked in the fields planting the new season's crops. Gregory met many people on his journey, kindly peasants who offered shelter in their steaming warm huts for the night, hungry pilgrims in ragged cloaks begging along the roadside, tax collectors hunting their prey, and Cossacks on horseback carrying sabres and whips as they galloped proudly over the plains.

At last, many months later, on the marshes of the Neva river, St Petersburg came into sight, spreading across the islands. It was like a fairy-tale city, huge palaces of red and yellow and green and blue soaring skywards, and the gigantic Cathedral of Our Lady of Kazan dominating the city. How aptly it was named Babylon of the Snows, he thought, its fabulous towers rising above the white snow like a city one might conjure up in one's most exotic dreams.

He entered the city with wondering eyes, and was enamoured of its sweeping wide boulevards and ornately-planted gardens, the columns and canopies, the balconies and basilicas of its magnificent architecture. The many canals intersecting the city gleamed flatly under the bridges and snowflakes glinted on the rooftops, the air was alive with the sound of carriage wheels and people's voices and church bells and street vendors' cries. Gregory felt a tingling in his veins. This was where life was to be found, he could sense it. Life would begin anew for him here, in this as yet untried twentieth century.

For some months he stayed in the capital city, entranced by its beauty and majesty and revelling in the warm reception he enjoyed, for his reputation as a starets with strange powers had preceded him there. He wondered at the power of men's words, that news of his doings should have travelled from furthest Siberia before his arrival, and was flattered when Father John of Kronstadt, a venerable, saintly old man who had been confessor to the last Tsar, Alexander III, received him kindly.

They talked for hours and found that in their beliefs they had much in common. The old man's eyes shone with pleasure.

"And I also believe implicitly in the absolute authority of the Tsar," the old man averred.

"As I do myself," Gregory agreed.

The next day Gregory stood at the back of the cathedral and watched Father John celebrating the mass. The vast building was crowded with the pressing bodies of the faithful, and as Father John held high the Host as the moment of Communion approached, he called in a cracked treble to those about to communicate, "Approach in faith and in the fear of God."

Bodies began to move forward. "Stop!" the old man's voice cried, and the congregation watched in amazement as he put down the Host and beckoned to a ragged pilgrim with a beard to come forward.

Gregory came forward and bent on one knee. Father John made the Sign of the Cross over his head in blessing and then to everyone's amazement the old man fell stumblingly to his knees and besought the pilgrim to bless him in return.

"Who was he, the bearded pilgrim?" one asked another as the mass ended and the church emptied.

"Don't you know? It was Gregory Rasputin, the starets from Siberia."

"Then Father John must believe him to be a very holy man indeed, to ask his blessing."

"Indeed he is. Have you not heard that he is blessed with second sight? I heard he told those present at the shrine in Sarov that it had just been revealed to him that a new miracle was about to take place, and that a year would not elapse before an heir would be born to the Throne."

"That would indeed be a miracle, for there has been no male heir to the Throne for nearly three hundred years. And so far the Empress has succeeded in producing only four girls. It will be interesting to see whether this starets is right. Do you think he is truly holy and endowed with powers?"

"I have no doubt of it. My friend could tell you how the starets helped him walk again, simply by putting his hands on the crippled leg and bidding him walk. And there are many more, here in St Petersburg as well as in Siberia, who could testify to his powers."

Gregory, feeling highly contented with his phenomenal success in the city, left again after five months. He had not fared too badly, having been well rewarded by generous citizens for his intercessions on their behalf, and having been acknowledged by the powerful old man Father John, for he was a favourite of the Tsaritsa herself. Who knew, one day he might even introduce Gregory to the Empress Alexandra if he played his cards right.

For more than a year he wandered, praying and preaching, succouring the sick and curing them, and all the time his reputation grew. He paid a flying visit to Pokrovskoe and found the cradle now occupied by a dark-haired baby girl named Maria, while the placid Dimitri played contentedly on the floor near his mother. Gregory moved his wife and children into a larger house in the main street of Pokrovskoe, a fine house with a garden and a courtyard, and Praskovie opened her arms to her husband and smiled, then just as suddenly, he was gone.

Word came to him while he journeyed that the Empress had given birth to a son, the Tsarevitch Alexis, in August 1904. Gregory smiled. So his prognostication in Sarov had come true. He hoped the Royal couple in the midst of their jubilation would remember his prophecy and be glad. Perhaps now would be an opportune time to return to St Petersburg.

Father John welcomed him back joyfully, and arranged for Gregory to lodge in the guest house of the Theological Academy, which was directed by his close friend, the Archimandrite Theophan. Gregory agreed willingly, for Theophan was a trusted friend and favourite of the Empress also, having once been her confessor, and there could be in the whole of Russia no better sponsors for him than these two elderly and respected churchmen. He must take pains to earn this man's respect.

To his delight, Theophan too was impressed by Gregory's simple piety and air of penitence. Gregory sat and listened to the great man engrossed in religious debate with his students and learned much of theological principles. In time he began to enter the discussions with them, and Theophan's old eyes glowed with pleasure. Through him, Gregory earned the approval of Bishop Hermogen of Saratov also, and with the blessing of all these powerful Church Fathers, his entry into Russian society was assured.

Elegant drawing-rooms were suddenly eager to receive the Siberian starets, despite his filthy, shaggy appearance and his thick, flat-syllabled accent. Ladies of society vied for his presence at their tables and tried to ignore the farmyard smell that emanated from his unwashed body. He smiled to himself at their efforts to remain polite, for he himself had no inhibitions. He addressed everyone on equal terms, with none of the deference usually expected of a peasant for a boyar, one of the nobility.

The ordinary people, the workers and peasants, still came to him for help. One evening it was a pretty young wife who longed to bear her husband a child, but so far with no success. She pleaded with Gregory to intercede for her.

"One prayer, master, one prayer from your holy lips should do the trick. Or lay your hands on my belly that I may conceive quickly," she pleaded earnestly.

Gregory resisted with difficulty the pang of desire that inflamed his body. She was a firm and shapely young woman, and given five minutes alone with her he could have guaranteed what she desired. But he fought the feeling down resolutely, and knelt and prayed with her.

Once she had gone, her eyes ashine with hope, Gregory

pondered his way of life. It was very restricting to live in the Theological Academy with all those future priests. If he wanted to remain free to pursue all his desires, he must move to where he would no longer be under surveillance.

Then he met George Sassonoff, a young journalist sharing a house with several other young people.

"You are welcome to a flat in my house," George said amiably, and Gregory leapt at the opportunity. Now, with a flat of his own in St Petersburg, he could do as he wished.

And opportunities presented themselves lavishly, Although he could see the noses of refined ladies sniff disdainfully when he entered a salon, he did not trouble to wash himself. More often than not he slept in his day clothes, rose and went to bed again still in the same garments. The stink of sweat did not trouble him, nor did it the fine ladies he noticed after a time. They became so entranced by his face that they forgot all else.

Rasputin searched his face carefully in the mirror. It was his eyes, yes, that was it, for since his childhood people had remarked on his eyes. They *were* rather striking, set in an otherwise unremarkable face, with their unusual brilliance and penetration. He stared at himself and watched the pupils retract until they almost disappeared.

Odd that, but whatever the light, brilliant or twilight, it seemed he could expand and contract the black pupils as he willed. He watched and tried again, opening and closing the curtains against the bright sunlight in turns. Yes, he could! Even in near-darkness, when a pupil was usually at its widest, he could narrow his to minute, menacing pinpoints. Was that what fascinated the people he met? Was that what gave him the power to be able to dictate to them?

And if so, how far could he carry out his mastery over them? Would he be able, say, to persuade someone to do some act which was against his principles, merely by talking to him while gazing at him with this steady, fixed look?

It would be interesting to experiment and find out. Rasputin decided to put it to the test when next the opportunity occurred.

NINE

SEVEN years had elapsed since Gregory Rasputin first left his wife and village to come to St Petersburg, and in the meantime she had borne him two daughters, Maria and Varvara. Rasputin paid occasional swift visits to her and took delight in seeing his young family grow and how well-respected they were by the village folk for their fine house and celebrated father. He saw to it that Praskovie received a liberal amount of the money that was given to him by people grateful for his help, and left again to continue his career in the capital.

The atmosphere of the great city excited him, composed as it was of so many elements. The greatest artists and musicians in the world flourished there, and the city abounded with concerts and operas and ballets. The rich people lived in a frenzy of excitement, drinking and gambling, visiting brothels, having wild and voluptuous affairs and killing and committing suicide with sensual abandon. They seemed oblivious to the starving, ragged millions of the working classes whose gaunt eyes watched the delirious antics of their betters with cold, detached hatred. Rasputin watched in fascination. It seemed incredible that the nobles, so few of Russia's population, could enjoy such extremes of luxury while the teeming millions died of want and hunger unnoticed. The upper classes deluded themselves that all Russians loved the Tsar and therefore would cause him no trouble.

But from what Rasputin learnt from café-table conversations and dropped hints in salons, the Tsar, Nicholas II, was no longer universally believed to be infallible. Despite family opposition, he had insisted on marrying the German princess he loved, Alix of Hesse-Darmstadt, ten years ago, and since that day she had kept him closeted in his family and his people no longer knew him.

He was reputed to be weak too, easily persuaded by his ministers and then rapidly changing his mind again. Only last year, 1904, he had let Plehve, Minister of the Interior, persuade him to go to war with Japan over Korean and Manchurian territory, with the disastrous result that he had had to surrender Port Arthur and then Mukden and finally suffered the indignity of having the Russian fleet annihilated by the Japanese at Tsushima.

The revolutionaries in Russia made capital out of the Tsar's mistakes and lost no time in pointing out to the starving Russian peasants what feeble leadership they had from him. The millions were becoming restless. Already the signs were there, but the rich went on dancing and drinking and debauching blindly.

One incident which showed Rasputin the measure of the workers' discontent and the total disinterest of the nobility was a snowy January march of thousands of workers, led by a priest named Father Gapon. Rasputin watched the ragged herd, led by the shouting, gesticulating priest, as they marched on the Winter Palace to present a petition on behalf of the Russian people.

Thousands of workers from all over Russia, including the men on strike from the Putilov steel works, converged and were joined by yet more of the peasants from within the city. An ice-cold wind drove flurries of snow into the faces, half-buried in their turned-up collars, and Gapon cried out to them encouragingly.

"Come, my friends! The Tsar will come out on the balcony and hear our plea, and as Father of Russia he will listen and deliver us from the oppressor. Come, lift your banners high!"

They listened and hoisted their banners and ikons wearily and trudged on. Rasputin caught a glimpse of a woman's face, white and peaked, but she had passed in the crowd before he could pin down the flicker of half-recognition.

Father Gapon began singing a hymn, and thousands of hoarse voices took up the tune. Rasputin watched. Thousands of faces of the Tsar wavered by on countless banners, and the peasants locked arms in a solid phalanx as they passed him in the direction of the Winter Palace.

It would serve them little purpose, he mused. No one cared for the plight of the serf. Petitions were useless. One day, perhaps, if they used the resources of their strength and numbers, they could right their wrongs, but pleading was futile.

He began to turn his footsteps homewards, but a sudden volley of gunfire caused him to halt suddenly. He looked back. The Cossacks had opened fire on the advancing horde, and the line wavered. Bodies fell as bullet shots ripped through the air and voices began to scream. Rasputin saw women clutching their children in horror as bodies began to blotch the snow-white ground with creeping crimson stains. Then they all began to run, and the Cossack gunfire pursued them. Father Gapon was miraculously the first fleeing figure to pass him. Then a woman came stumbling by.

"Help me, for God's sake, help me! My husband is shot!"

She clung to Rasputin's sleeve, her eyes wide with terror and pleading. A lurch of recognition suddenly recalled her to him—it was the girl from Pokrovskoe—Tanya—but a woman now, no longer a girl.

"Come with me." He grabbed her arm and ran, seconds

before the fleeing multitude engulfed them. Crushed by the panic-stricken bodies, it was difficult to remain upright, but at last they found themselves in a deserted side street near Rasputin's flat. Without hesitation he took her in.

She watched him while he made hot tea for them both, her eyes vacant.

"You remember me, Tanya?" he asked at last.

"Yes. You are Gregory Efimovitch, or Rasputin as they call you now."

"Why are you here in St Petersburg?"

"Boris—my husband—wanted to join Father Gapon's petition march. Now he is dead."

"Boris? You married Boris Mikhailovitch?"

She nodded slowly. "Seven years ago. He was a good husband, and now . . ."

"Are you sure he's dead? Perhaps he was only wounded."

"A bullet hit him between the eyes. He is dead. And innocent women and children lie dead in the street, too. The Tsar does not care for us. No one cares for such as us."

Her voice held the flat, expressionless tone of a woman in a trance. Rasputin turned away. She must pull herself together. Death and misery were no novelty to peasants, but a daily hazard they all faced. She must accept it and begin again.

After a time, she slept, upright in the chair. When she awoke, she still showed no sign of tears, but only a blank, bewildered look.

"Tell me, what shall I do now, Gregory?"

For the first time, she turned her eyes full upon him. Rasputin looked back at her fixedly.

"You must begin life anew, Tanya. Have you children at home, or family?"

She shook her head. "Our only child died in infancy. And my grandmother is dead. I am alone."

"Then you could stay here in St Petersburg and find work."

She shook her head. Her stare was still vacant. Rasputin narrowed his pupils deliberately and gazed deeply into her eyes.

"Tanya, do you hear me?" She nodded. "You will go to the inn at the corner and ask for work, you hear me?"

"I—I feel drowsy, Gregory. I cannot think."

"Tell me how you feel."

"My body feels numb. I can see nothing but your eyes, Gregory—two beautiful shining lights before my face, and nothing else."

"Do you feel my hands?" He bent over her and slid his palms across her knees. She did not move."

"I—I don't know. I feel a warmth tingling through me, that is all. And your eyes are deep and dark now. I am so sleepy, so tired."

He slid his hands up across her bodice, under her cloak and inside her frock, feeling the firm contours of her breasts. She did not flinch, but continued to stare blankly into his eyes.

"Tanya," he said in a low, husky voice, his lips almost touching her hair, "you will go to ask for work at the inn, will you not?"

"Yes, Gregory." Her reply was no more than a faint whisper. Rasputin withdrew his hands and stood back.

"Good, then that is settled. You may sleep here if you wish until you find an apartment of your own."

Tanya stayed, from the Bloody Sunday until some weeks later when her work at the inn had produced sufficient money for her to share a cramped little room with another barmaid. But in that time, Rasputin could not bring himself to seduce her. Other women were fair game and well-nigh offered him

70

their virtue when they sought his help and he had no compunction about availing himself of their services, but Tanya was different. Pleasures of the flesh were part of Rasputin's beliefs; after all, he had found nothing in the Scriptures to refute it, but Tanya was still the child he had known, innocent and part of his youth. He could not touch her.

She was comely enough as a woman in her mid-twenties should be, but she still had a reverent attitude towards him as she had as a child. No doubt she would have succumbed easily if he had taken her to bed with him, but there was no joy or achievement in bedding a child who regarded him as a saint.

And in any event, other matters occupied Rasputin's mind. The unrest before Bloody Sunday was simmering more rapidly now. Ninety-two Russian workers lay dead in the snow and more than two hundred were wounded. No one seemed to care but the Russian peasants, who grew bitter and more determined to seek justice. The Tsar's uncle, the Grand Duke Serge, was assassinated in Moscow only three weeks later. Workers all over Russia went on strike and murdered policemen, the battleship Potemkin's crew mutinied over the rotten meat they were given to eat, and by autumn St Petersburg itself was in a state of siege. A nationwide strike paralysed the country. Ships lay idle, no trains ran, hospitals and schools closed down, and no food or newspapers could be obtained in the city.

But the richer citizens of the capital danced and feasted on frenetically, stubbornly ignoring the chaos in the countryside beyond, where starving peasants robbed and maimed, set fire to the noble houses and raided their estates. Surely, they reasoned, the peasants would quieten down before long.

It was at this point that Rasputin, already accepted by most of the influential people in St Petersburg, met the Grand

Duchesses Militsa and Stana. He was not slow to notice the gleam in Militsa's eye when she proffered her hand. She was obviously entranced with him. Rasputin chuckled aloud. She would be the means of his next advancement, he promised himself.

TEN

THE Grand Duchess Militsa was fascinated by the disreputable-looking creature who advanced coolly into her salon. He looked just as a holy man should—cheap, coarse, peasant shirt knotted round with a piece of rope, baggy and filthy breaches, and leather boots which had obviously seen many better days. Truly a man of soul, not given to caring about worldly luxury.

He greeted her casually, as though she were not one of the highest nobles in the land. Militsa was delighted. So he was not trying to curry favour with her because of her position. One could forgive the vile smell that drifted from his armpits and ruined the delicate scent of her salon, for he was undoubtedly a very special starets indeed.

"You are most welcome to my house, Rasputin," she said graciously. Many would give their eye teeth for such an acclamation, for were not she and her sister Stana both "the Montenegrins", daughters of King Nikita and now wives of the Grand Dukes Peter and Nicolai Nicolaievitch? And had not Militsa been one of the Empress's closest friends after nursing her through an illness? Militsa tried hard to forget the estrangement that had grown between herself and Alexandra since Militsa's fervent interest in spiritualism had turned the pious Empress against her.

But the ragged holy man standing before her, leaning casually on one of her most elegant French wine tables and helping himself to her wine, seemed to know nothing of the proprieties. He was insolent enough to mention that which was never mentioned.

"I understand you and the Empress are no longer friendly," he stated boldly. "Why is that?"

Militsa flushed a little. She was not accustomed to having to answer for her actions to mere peasants, but the direct and searching look in his cold grey eyes demanded honest reply. He was the holy man all St Petersburg was talking of, the miracle-worker who was gifted with rare abilities, and no matter how one might be repelled by his filthy appearance one remembered that fact. Moreover, those eyes demanded instant compliance.

"Why is that?" he repeated coolly.

Militsa smiled to cover her embarrassment. "The Empress was indeed a good friend of mine, as you say, and still is to some measure, but I fear she disapproves of our interest in spiritual matters." It was only a half-answer, and Militsa was aware of Rasputin's keenly quizzical look inviting more. She hesitated before going on.

"She took a keen interest at first in our little séances and our table-tapping, but then she changed her mind. Maybe she feared she would see a table rise in the air, or maybe her priestly advisers warned her against it, I know not, but she ceased to participate and no longer visits us."

"I see." Rasputin rubbed his shaggy beard with a grimy forefinger thoughtfully. He seemed quite unaware of the many eyes in the salon watching him keenly. It was not often they saw such a beggarly figure amid the fine French furnishings and heavy, ornate hangings of this luxurious room.

"But I am still admitted to the Royal presences," Militsa said defensively. "Do not believe that I am ostracised."

"But she does not approve of your dabbling with mysticism." Militsa heard the disapproval in his voice and rushed to defend herself.

"I only wanted to help her! It was she who begged me to

find some way to help her conceive a male child, an heir to the throne. I told her of a French holy man I had heard of who was reputed to be able to work wonders, and took him to her."

"And how did she receive him?"

"Philippe Vachot? She welcomed him, for she was beginning to give up hope after bearing three girls. She certainly became pregnant again quickly."

"And bore a fourth daughter," Rasputin murmured. "As he is no longer at Court, I presume she then dismissed him."

"Not then," Militsa admitted quietly. "He assured her her next child would be a boy. She trusted him implicitly and when he told her she was again pregnant, she believed it. Why, even her stomach grew fat and she was sick in the mornings, but as time went on, her own doctor examined her and found she was not pregnant at all. Then she sent Vachot away."

Militsa wondered why she was telling all this to the unkempt creature, a matter she almost never referred to nowadays, but still the steel-grey eyes were fixed on her and she could do nothing but speak the truth. It was with a feeling of great relief, however, that she saw her husband enter the salon and cross the room to join them.

"Peter Nicolaievitch, where have you been for so long? I want to introduce to you Gregory Rasputin, of whom all St Petersburg is talking."

She smiled graciously and watched the peasant figure ignore her husband's proffered hand and simply nod curtly. Peter hastened to explain his absence.

"It was Caesar—my favourite hound. He is sick, and I think it's the end of him. I've been with him this last hour, but his breathing grows worse. I fear he will not live till morning."

Before Militsa could murmur words of sympathy, the ragged starets looked quickly at her husband.

"Let me see the dog," he rasped.

Peter's eyes widened fractionally, and then he led Rasputin out. Half an hour later he returned, his eyes shining with pleasure.

"But where is Rasputin?" his wife asked, regretful at having lost her distinguished guest.

"He said he was going to the gypsy camp at Novaya Derevnya, for he felt in need of an hour of singing and dancing. But he cured Caesar, Militsa! It's incredible, but he simply knelt and laid his dirty hands on the beast, muttered a few words I couldn't hear, and the dog just went to sleep, breathing normally!"

"There! Didn't I tell you he was a miracle-worker!" Militsa breathed triumphantly. "Now do you believe me?"

"I wouldn't have—but I saw with my own eyes!"

"Then let us tell our guests." She could barely wait to let it be known. The Grand Duchess Militsa entertained none but the most outstanding and scintillating people at her soirées.

Long after all the guests had departed Militsa was alone with her husband in their bedroom.

"Help me unbutton my gown, my dear," she said. As Peter's thin fingers fiddled awkwardly, she murmured casually, "Don't you think it might be a good idea, my love, if I were to introduce Rasputin at Court?"

Peter's fingers suddenly stopped. "Would that be wise, after Vachot?"

Militsa clicked her tongue with annoyance. "Well, the Empress did give birth to a son soon after he left, did she not? Alexis is fifteen months old now. No, what I was thinking was that since the baby is so often ill, maybe Rasputin could cure

76

him as he did Caesar. The Empress might well have cause to be grateful to me after all."

Peter sighed as he unfastened the last buttons. "At any other time I should forbid it, Militsa, but after what I have seen tonight . . ."

"Then that is settled. I shall simply introduce him, let the Empress know of his magical powers, and leave the rest up to her. There's no harm in that, is there?"

Peter yawned. "None at all, as far as I can see."

Rasputin strode homeward towards his apartment in the crisp snow, glistening white under the moonlight. God, but what a merry night it had been! It was wonderful to escape from the stifling, confined atmosphere of the Grand Duchess Militsa's salon to the carefree, lusty atmosphere of the gypsies' camp by the riverside. What drinking and singing there had been, and a dusky voluptuous gypsy wench to round it off pleasantly. She had looked into his eyes, glistening in the firelight, and had needed no second invitation. Such vigour, such strong, passionate responsiveness in her sleek body! It was an enjoyable night indeed, when human senses could be savoured to the full. This was what life was for, to feel and experience all that the body was capable of.

And there was the added delicious thought that maybe he had started off a train of events in Militsa's mind, for he knew he had played his cards well there. It was a stroke of luck about the dog. One word from Militsa to the Empress, who was reputed to be very impressionable, and with luck he could find himself at Court!

Rasputin could not resist skipping for a step or two, sending up flurries of snow about him. It was an exciting prospect. It was not that he wanted to gain any material benefits from the Tsar and the Empress, only that he wanted to be recognised by them. Already he had conquered Pokrovskoe, then

Siberia and now St Petersburg, but to be acclaimed as a man of power by royalty themselves—what a cachet that would be! All the world would come to know of Gregory Rasputin, the holy man! People the world over would seek him out. He gloried in the prospect.

He belched noisily as he turned the corner of the deserted street. Surprising really that he was not drunk, after the many flagons he had consumed tonight. His stomach lining must be growing hardened to the wine, he thought, for he scarcely ever became drunk nowadays, however liberally he imbibed.

At the doorway to his apartment he stopped. Across the road two men lurked in the shadows and drew further back at his approach. Were the secret police still watching him since Father Peter denounced him at Pokrovskoe so long ago? Rasputin pushed the thought from his mind and mounted the stairs.

Two figures huddled in cloaks stood against the wall in the gloom outside his door. Rasputin hesitated. One was a man, the other a woman. He sighed. Yet more people looking for his help, he thought. All day people came knocking, sometimes filling the staircase as they waited, but in the middle of the night . . .

The man moved forward. "Starets, I came only to thank you for your prayers for my child. She recovered instantly. God bless you—and please take this. It is all I have."

He disappeared quickly down the stairs, leaving Rasputin to gaze at the few kopeks he had pushed into his hand. The woman approached timidly.

"Holy father, I beg you to spare a prayer for me. I am a widow with five small children and the landlord will throw us out if I do not pay the rent. But I cannot. Pray our Blessed Virgin to intercede for me."

Rasputin nodded, lowered his head and muttered a few

words which he knew she could not understand. Then he raised his head and gazed at her meaningfully.

"Take this, good woman, and go home and sleep in peace."

She stared disbelievingly at the handful of kopeks he placed in her hand. "It is a miracle! God be praised!" She sank on her knees before him and reached for his hand, but Rasputin drew it away.

"Go home to your children," he muttered, and passed by her into his apartment.

ELEVEN

THE Tsar, Nicholas II, Emperor of all the Russias, lay fully dressed on the double bed and listened to the running bath water in the room next door where his wife was preparing for her evening bath.

He had been busy in his study this last three hours, receiving a constant stream of callers, giving audiences and conversing with his ministers, and now he was tired. Soon it would be time for family supper, and Alexandra always insisted on the full formality of evening dress and jewels although there would be no guests, just themselves and the older children.

Nicholas rubbed the back of his hand across his smarting eyes. He was tired, and his cares seemed to grow heavier day by day. He sighed, sat up and lit another cigarette. Alexandra would object to the smell of smoke in the bedroom, but it would help to alleviate his tension.

He could not help feeling resentful. He had never wanted to be Tsar, but Fate had decreed otherwise and the cares of State were oppressively heavy for one man alone. He looked at himself in Alex's long pier glass. He was too slight in build, too gentle-eyed to follow in the footsteps of Ivan the Terrible, Peter the Great and even his own father, Alexander III. He just was not framed to be an all-powerful autocrat, the demi-god the Russian millions worshipped. He recalled with envy the carefree days of his youth when he led the life of an irresponsible rake, then the energetic, joyful days of his army life, and then the blissful days when he had fallen in love with a beautiful golden-haired German princess.

Gone were those carefree days now. He had wooed and won his German beauty, the Princess Alix of Hesse-Darmstadt, despite separation and parental opposition, only because his stern mother had relented as her husband lay dying. And the only reason for her submission was because Russia now needed a new Tsar, and young Nicholas would be the better able to rule if embedded in a stable marriage. Thus the joy Nicholas anticipated in his marriage coincided with having the cares of the Crown thrust upon him, and life had never flowed easily since.

Their marriage was undoubtedly a success, he thought, flicking cigarette ash into the tray. The love she had first inspired in him was mutual and still flourished. They lived for each other, and tried as far as possible to shut out the rest of the world except their children. Of all Nicholas's eight palaces they had chosen this one, Tsarskoe Selo, the least pretentious despite its hundred rooms, as their main home, and had allotted the main portion to be state chambers, one wing to be apartments for ministers and the like, and the remaining wing was their own private world where no one but family and servants penetrated.

He smiled as he recalled their early married days. Alexandra had grimaced but made no comment, but he had known nevertheless that she hated sharing the Anitchkov Palace with his mother, the Dowager Empress Marie. Mother was charming enough, but the young couple could never find occasion to be alone together unless they slipped out and away by night on a horse-drawn sleigh across the crisply snow-strewn city.

And then with the advent of their first child they had escaped to Tsarskoe Selo. It was a haven of retreat, a place they could be alone together and at peace. Although the baby had disappointingly proved to be a girl, they had been blissfully happy alone, just he and Alex and baby Olga.

He stubbed out his cigarette. The door to the bathroom opened and Alex appeared from the mists of steam, her still-slender figure wrapped in a gay kimono.

"Day-dreaming, my dear?" she asked. She still had the smooth skin and unlined face of a young girl untrammelled by care. Nicholas marvelled at her placid patience. "What are you thinking of?"

"Oh—just remembering. I was thinking how carefree we were at the Coronation." He stretched out full-length on the bed again, his hands behind his head, and watched her unpin her long golden hair and begin to brush it with long, smooth strokes.

"You are not worrying over dropping the Order of St Andrew on the altar steps, are you, just because some said it was an evil omen?"

"No, of course not, my love. I leave the mysticism and superstition to you."

He noticed that with her usual diplomacy she did not mention the other omen—the accidental death of three thousand of his subjects at Khodinski Fields as they celebrated his coronation. It still caused him a pang to recall how the boards had given way, plunging his people into a trench, and how the massed, jubilating crowd had pushed on, trampling their comrades to death unwittingly. That had been a terrible omen indeed.

She turned large eyes upon him. "Are you mocking me, Nicholas?"

"Never!" He leapt up and came to put his hands on her shoulders, looking at the lovely face in the mirror. His finger-tips caressed her hair. "How beautiful you are, Alex! One would never guess what cares you suffer."

He turned away abruptly and lit another cigarette. He had not wanted to remind her of baby Alexis's illness for he knew

82

how she suffered a mother's agony already. He stubbed out the cigarette again angrily. How frustrating it was not to be able to lift the burden from her gentle shoulders. God knew how he worried himself about the boy's illness, but he wished fiercely that there was some way he could help poor Alex in her misery.

He prodded his toe gingerly into the pile of the mauve carpet, Alex's favourite colour. "How is Alexis today?" he asked tentatively. It was a question he feared to ask, because daily the child, an energetic toddler of three now, ran the risk of a minor knock which could mean death. Haemophilia, the doctors called it. What an affliction for an innocent child, and even more so when the child was the future Emperor of Russia —if he lived long enough to acquire the title.

"Thank God, he is well," the Empress sighed. She turned and surveyed her husband, still wearing the peasant smock and baggy trousers he habitually wore in his study, and smiled. "Why do you wear these clothes and not an impressive uniform?" she asked.

"I feel is helps me identify with my people, After all, they do call me Batiushka, Little Father."

"And me Matushka, but I fear it means little for they have no feeling for me," she picked up the brush and began stroking her hair again languidly. He knew what she meant. The people had made it obvious that they cared little for a foreign princess as their Empress, and even less when she lured their Tsar away from his State duties and tried to involve him only in their domestic life.

"Nonsense, my dear," he tried to reassure her. "How could they help but be impressed by your beauty and grace? And they know what a splendid wife and mother you are."

"Then why do you need to place such a heavy guard on me when I ride out in the carriage in the afternoons? Two grooms, two footmen, the coachman and a Cossack officer go with me always."

"It is no more than any lady of rank is entitled to, my dear." Nicholas refrained from pointing out that the police too had their eye on her when she rode out, that every bush and tree she passed had a vigilant officer strategically placed behind it and that no one she spoke to could return to his home before stringent cross-examination had cleared him of suspicion. His wife was not popular in the country, but Nicholas would never dream of admitting it to her. He loved her too much to want to add to her worry. In their own private world of love and warmth they could give each other the security they both so badly needed.

Alex rose and went into her dressing-room. When she emerged, resplendent in a magnificent gown that showed her shapely bare shoulders, jewels gleaming at her throat and ears, Nicholas was already bathed and dressed.

"A moment in the chapel, Nicky dear, before we go down to supper," Alex said with a shy smile, and led the way into the little room opening off their bedroom. It was a stark little room, bare of all but a table on which a Bible lay open and a gold ikon on one wall. It had the hushed and reverent air of a chapel, dimly lit as it was by hanging lamps. Alex knelt before the ikon and closed her eyes. Nicholas bowed his head behind her and prayed too. His prayers entreated help in State matters, but he knew hers would be centred solely on the baby son she adored.

Then he took her arm and led her out, along polished corridors where red-caped equerries with plumed hats bowed as they passed and white-gaitered footmen hurried before them to open doors. Through drawing-rooms and ante-rooms they glided silently, over parquet and deep luxurious carpets, till they reached the dining-room. A pair of lackeys with scarlet scarves about their heads caught up with metal clasps bowed low and opened the doors wide for the royal pair.

The children were waiting. Nicholas smiled to see Olga, the eldest and closest to his heart, for she was so like himself. She was twelve now and the promise of beauty was already there in the long chestnut tresses and the gentle blue eyes. Beside her Tatiana curtseyed to her parents gracefully. She was the one most like her mother, the lively, energetic head with its auburn gold curls and deep grey eyes seeming a more vivacious version of Alexandra though she was but ten years old.

"I shall play the piano to you after supper," she told her parents with a grin. Olga frowned. "You mean *may* you play the piano. You shouldn't be so bossy, Tatiana."

Maria, only a year younger than Tatiana, tossed her light brown hair and turned her deep blue eyes on her father. A merry laugh lingered behind the eyes, he noticed as she spoke. "But Tatiana will play, won't she, Father? She always gets her own way. Now when I'm a mother, I shall be very stern with my children."

Olga smiled good-humouredly. "She talks of nothing else but when she's married and has children. You'd think she was nineteen, not nine."

Anastasia, the youngest, opened her blue eyes wide. "Well, I'm only six and I like playing at being Mama with my dolls. What's wrong with that?" Nicholas guessed, though he could not see, that she was nudging Maria, for he saw Maria's enquiring look at her. Anastasia was the playful one amongst them, the tomboy given to witticisms and practical joking and she was undoubtedly trying to make her big sister Olga rise to the bait now. Alexandra intervened.

"Hush now, darlings. Tell me what you have done today." Earnest young voices began to prattle about their lessons and their tutors, especially Pierre Gilliard, the French tutor, about their beloved Dr Botkin, the Court physician who examined them daily, about their walk in the park with their English collie dogs, about their new dresses and sashes which had just arrived, but Nicholas saw that his wife's dreamy expression indicated that her thoughts were drifting. To the nursery upstairs, no doubt, where the young Tsarevitch sat in his cot waiting for her regular evening visit to say good night.

"My dress is exactly the same as Olga's," Tatiana was complaining to her mother.

"And mine is the same as Anastasia's," Maria said indignantly. "I don't think a girl of nine should have to wear the same as a little six-year-old."

"But I like the big pair to be dressed alike, and the young pair too," Alex explained. "It looks very attractive, don't you think so too, Papa?"

Nicholas smiled and nodded. If only his whole life could be centred on this family group he could be a happy man indeed, he mused, despite little Alexis's condition. There was such love and warmth and closeness here. What a pity he had to involve himself with State and business matters which took up far too much of his time and energy. It would be so peaceful to be as other men.

The meal ended, Alex rose and smiled at her daughters. "Now go and prepare for bed, there's good girls. Our good friend Rasputin has promised to look in to say good night to you all."

Four young faces lit up eagerly. The Empress turned to her husband and took his arm. "Let us send all the servants away and our little family and our friend can enjoy each other's company more intimately alone, can we not?"

Nicholas nodded. This Rasputin fellow might not be a very

charming character in his eyes, but he certainly brought a rare smile of hope to Alex's lovely face.

"Very well, my dear. Dismiss the servants and call me from my study when Rasputin arrives."

Nicholas kissed his daughters and left. He welcomed the thought of a pleasant chat with Rasputin this evening. Such a good, honest, simple-minded fellow was a welcome change from devious ministers and one could speak freely and be at one's ease with him. How refreshing to have a friend who thought only of heavenly matters, free from the scheming ambitions of lesser men.

TWELVE

ALEXANDRA watched proudly while the tall figure of the Siberian holy man bent over her youngest child, and saw the boy's face light up as the fairy tale Rasputin was telling him reached its climax. The girls, all dressed in their white nightgowns and with their hair tumbling loose, listened with rapt attention and Alexandra could not help reflecting that in the light of the candles which burned before the ikons they looked like pure young angels surrounding the figure of a saint.

When he had done, Alexandra listened to the young Tsarevitch say his prayers and then tucked him up for the night.

"You should visit us more often, Rasputin," she chided the holy man gently as they sat together later in the drawing-room. "They love to listen to you, and Nicholas and I enjoy your company so much."

"I shall try, Matushka, but my work keeps me occupied."

"Of course, I am sorry. I should not forget that you have much to do to help the poor and heal the sick. I bless the day Militsa brought you to us, dear friend. Was it but two years ago? But I must not forget that others need you. I hear that there are always queues at your door."

Rasputin spread his hands. "One does what one can."

And he had done much for her, Alexandra reflected later in her bedroom as she undressed. In the past two years he had been a source of great comfort and solace to her. A friend indeed, someone who asked no return for the spiritual balm he brought to her wounded soul. So patient, so gentle, despite his uncouth appearance. He was indeed a very holy man, too devout to care about worldly acquisitions. Why, his lodging was a humble one, and his clothes showed his disinterest in material things. But one could not judge by appearances. His soothing words from the Scriptures, his kindly concern and familiar habit of taking her hands as he spoke to her, all these were the signs of true friendship. She was lucky to have a starets as her friend, for God knew how she needed friendship.

Alexandra sighed. Life had not been easy these last thirteen years, since the day she had married her beloved Nicky. The House of the Romanovs was reputed to be doomed, and so far the legend was borne out. Nicky's grandfather, Alexander II, had died treacherously, slain by an assassin's bomb, and his father, Alexander III, had died at the age of only forty-eight. Only after four girls had she and her husband succeeded in producing a son, little Alexis, but he had fallen victim to the Romanov curse in inheriting this terrible disease.

Alexandra flinched, as she always did when she thought of her son's strange illness. How was she to know, when she fell in love with Nicky that she carried in her veins this terrible thing she transmitted to her beloved boy. It was her fault. She, in her ignorance, had given him this blight. And now she had to watch him suffer. No one had known of the evil thing until he was six weeks' old, when his navel would not stop haemorrhaging. That had been the first indication that all was not well.

Nicholas arrived just as Alexandra climbed into bed. His normally sad face wore a smile.

"Fine fellow, that Rasputin. So reassuring and at the same time so unassuming."

"I know just what you mean, Nicky. He calms my fears too."

"Come now, sweetheart. What are you frightened of?" She

could hear the false gaiety in his voice, the intention to reassure her that all was well, but she was a sensitive, intelligent woman. She knew the distant tremors that rocked the Throne and threatened their very existence. She knew of her own unpopularity with the Russian people, those silent, staring, menacing figures who surrounded her husband constantly, but she trusted none of them, nor they her. She knew misfortune dogged the Romanov footsteps, and dear little Alexis was an instance of it. Her eyes filled with tears.

"Beloved." Nicholas's voice was strangled. He had seen the tears and undressed quickly, cradling her close in his arms. "Do not be afraid, my darling. So long as we and our children are together, we are happy, are we not?"

"Yes." The word was lost in the hollow of his arm. Doubt haunted the Empress. But for how long? she longed to cry out. How long can we enjoy the love of our family securely? Much as she adored her husband, she knew his limitations. He was as ambitious as his father had been, but he lacked the strength and stature of Alexander to carry out his exploits. He had the will, but not the talent nor the strength.

And Nicholas himself shared her doubts and fears, she knew. He had been upset over the massacre of Bloody Sunday and had demanded in vain who was responsible. Events politically were becoming beyond his control, and he feared that some day soon another Father Gapon would become the focal point of the people's unrest, perhaps a man who was better able to channel their powers.

Nicholas heard her sniffing back her tears, and misinterpreted their meaning. "Do not fret for Alexis, my precious. I shall see to it he does not harm himself. In fact, I have appointed a man I trust to be by his side always, wherever he goes, to catch him if he should slip or fall. He cannot come to harm with Derevenko by his side."

"Derevenko? The sailor?"

"Yes. He is big and strong and will protect him well, for the child is too young yet to understand the risk he runs. Derevenko is to be trusted to guard him well. Sleep in peace now, beloved."

But the Empress could not rest. Sleeping and waking, her thoughts dwelt on her vulnerable child, and the sense of guilt pounded through her brain. However her husband comforted her, Alexandra knew she was to blame, however innocently, and believed her constant worry now was the punishment sent to her by God.

It was a long time before Nicholas fell asleep too. His mind was seething with the thoughts that were never far away and which Alexandra had just reawakened. The boy was always at risk, despite Derevenko or any other precaution, for he was by nature a tomboy. The angelic blue eyes and golden hair belied the daredevil temperament within, and although Alexis was only three, he was full of mischief and hard to control. However sharply Derevenko and the child's nurses were exhorted to watch over him, he must on some occasion give them the slip and hurt himself.

It was so ridiculous, really. A bump or a bruise which would normally not bother another child could trigger off the most terrible bleeding in Alexis. If it was a scratch, that could be suppressed by cold compresses and pressure, but if it was an internal bruise, the child was in agony. Nicholas had watched helplessly many a time when the bruise, usually surrounding a joint, had swollen and gone blue and made the boy scream with pain. That was when poor Alexanadra looked most piteous, wringing her hands and utterly unable to help him. Poor Alexandra. She felt the frustration worse than he did, feeling herself responsible.

Not that his own heart did not bleed for the boy also. But

he had other cares to concern him. To calm his restless subjects, he had formed the first parliamentary Duma two years ago and then a second, and for a time this had quietened them, but now it was apparent they were growing restless again. He would have to take action again soon or his imperial sovereignty would be threatened. Moreover, he knew better than Alexandra did how unpopular she was with his people. From the very beginning she had been shy and withdrawn, a stranger in a foreign land and completely overshadowed by the dominating figure of his own mother, the Dowager Empress Marie. And since Marie had been reluctant to hand over her imperial position to her new daughter-in-law, it had come about that the reserved Alexandra had let Marie continue to dominate the royal scene.

It was a pity really. Alexandra had tried hard. She had abandoned her own religion and adopted that of the Eastern Orthodox Church in order to please, but despite her beauty and gentleness his people had not accepted her attempts. She was so embarrassingly shy, twitching and blushing constantly in company, that they had misinterpreted her discomfort for dislike. And instead of speaking Russian—or even in French as most society people did—she persisted in speaking English, since she had been educated in England. The people consequently referred to her jeeringly as the Anglitschanka, the Englishwoman.

Nor did the people like the fact that Alexandra and he lived so much in seclusion, tucked away in Tsarskoe Selo. They could not know that Alexandra lived only for her family, and that constant brooding over her son and her guilt was turning her into a neurotic woman who felt secure only when alone with her family.

She was becoming more and more melancholy day by day. Nicholas sighed. How could he put a stop to her endless prayers and fasting when the doctors had said the haemophilia was incurable? There was nothing he could do for her but wait and hope and comfort her. And hope that Derevenko would discharge his duties well.

But when the summer came, tragedy struck again. It was July, 1907. The Tsarevitch Alexis was playing in the palace gardens when, just for an instant, Derevenko's watchful eyes were diverted. He looked back to where Alexis was playing on a home-made cart, just in time to see him stumble and fall. The huge, bearded sailor darted forward to clutch him, but not quickly enough. Alexis fell over the edge of the cart, the corner of it catching him in the groin, and he sprawled full-length on the grass.

Derevenko snatched him up solicitously, but already the little boy's eyes were filling with tears. Derevenko ran with the child to the nursery and summoned the doctor. A lackey went to inform the Empress.

By the time Alexandra rushed to her son, her eyes wide with unspoken fear and her négligée still unfastened in her haste, the boy was lying in his bed in a darkened room, Dr Botkin bending over him.

Botkin straightened. The Empress bent over the cot and searched her son's face for signs of pain, but as yet he was only whimpering with the bruise. She looked at the doctor.

"It is a large bruise, Your Majesty, and by nightfall it will have spread if the bleeding continues. We must watch him carefully."

"Oh no!" Alexandra covered her face with her hands. She knew what agony lay in store, both for the little white-faced boy in the bed and for herself in her anxiety and helplessness. As the bruise swelled and the pain pounded through the little body, he would cry out for relief, begging his mother for help, and, as always before, she would be able to do nothing. Once more they would both suffer exquisite torture.

"Nick—oh, Nicky!" she cried. "Where is my husband?"

"His Majesty is away, inspecting the troops. He will return shortly."

"I had forgotten." Alexandra turned from the cot, her shoulders drooping in misery. She made for the haven of her chapel and knelt abjectly before the ikon. Only God could help her now.

Four days later, the young prince growing weaker with pain and so wracked by it that he was nearly unconscious, Alexandra was still praying for a miracle.

"Have mercy, O Lord, if not on me then on my helpless baby! I know I deserve this suffering for my guilt, but not Alexis! Dear God, have pity!"

How long she was on her knees on the cold floor she neither knew nor cared. Physical discomfort meant nothing—she would have cut off her right hand if it could have helped the boy. But by nightfall her prayers had averted none of what was inevitably to follow.

"His temperature is rising, Your Majesty," Botkin told her as she walked with difficulty back to the nursery. The cold floor of the chapel had brought on again her life-long trouble of sciatica. Alexis lay groaning and turning, trying to ease the pain that throbbed more and more mercilessly. This could be the time he was taken from them, Alexandra realised with a pang of terror. So many times he had lain at death's door and yet survived as by a miracle. This time God might not be so merciful.

She was kneeling at the bedside when Nicholas came up behind her.

"How is he, Alexandra?" His face was as white as her own.

She shook her head despairingly. "If the good Lord does

not relent . . . Oh, Nicky! We need intervention. For God's sake send for Rasputin! He is the only man I know who is saintly enough to be able to intercede for us!"

"But, Alexandra, the Bishop, Father John, your own prayers . . ."

"I know! I know! But none is so holy as Rasputin! God no longer listens to me, but He will to Rasputin! Send for him quickly, before it is too late!"

THIRTEEN

THE heat of midsummer in St Petersburg was intolerable. Even though Gregory opened wide the windows of his new house in the Nevsky Prospect, a gift from the admiring Grand Duchess Olga, the cool breezes that drifted in carried with them the noise of bells and street vendors and troika wheels which brought no peace. When the last of the suppliants waiting at his door had gone, Rasputin longed for the freedom and peace of the countryside, away from the heat and smells of the city.

So now he lay on the bank of the river, a cool, dark-eyed gypsy girl nestling in the hollow of his arm, and revelled in the shimmering heat haze that lay over the rippling water. It was late evening, but the air still held that pearly iridescence that gives the scene a dream-like quality. Rasputin lay, his eyes half-closed, and felt content. The gypsy girl was an energetic filly and he had served her well. She appeared to be sleeping now, and Rasputin let his thoughts wander.

He was content enough in St Petersburg, for his self-esteem was well nourished by those who sought him out constantly, believing in his infallibility. Princes and peasants alike saluted him respectfully as a holy man. Here he was now, in his mid-thirties, venerated and sought after, with a fine two-storeyed house on the finest boulevard and the knowledge that his wife and children lived well too.

He saw Praskovie and the children from time to time, but the need to return to St Petersburg quickly drew him back.

True, the peasants of Pokrovskoe lauded him, but the approval of the capital meant far more to him.

He chuckled and the girl moved but did not waken. It had been a clever move on his part to become a pilgrim and then a starets, all those years ago. A holy man, a man of the cloth, was accepted by everyone. A mere peasant could never hope to cross the intangible but nevertheless impregnable barrier between the classes, but a holy man knew no class barriers. It had been at Verkhoture, so long ago, that he had first been shrewd enough to spot this fact.

Unlike Petcherkine, however, who stayed to become a priest on Mount Athos, he had been reluctant to spend all those years taking vows and praying and fasting, and then waiting and hoping for preferment. This way he had reached the top, accepted by the highest Church prelates like Father John and Bishop Hermogen, and even the Tsar and Tsarina themselves.

It satisfied his vanity that, in spite of his peasant origins, his ability and cleverness were recognised by the highest people in the land. This was power; this was what he had longed for in those early confining days in Pokrovskoe. Now he could come and go to the Winter Palace when he pleased, knowing he would be welcomed with delight. And never did he have to address the Emperor and Empress with a servile "Your Majesty". From the outset he had set the pattern by being familiar with them, and yet respectful, calling them Batiushka and Matushka, Little Father and Little Mother of their people. That was power.

The Tsarina, he knew, was more susceptible to his commanding manner than the Tsar. She trusted him implicitly, confiding in him even her most personal secrets. He was one of the few who knew of the Tsarevitch's hereditary illness, a secret which was kept from most of the world, even the boy's tutor. Moreover, he had been careful always to impress Anna

Vyrubova, the mild, plain and not over-intelligent woman who was the Empress's only close friend, and her constant words in his praise could not fail to be of help to him in that quarter.

He smiled to himself. Women were always more susceptible to his manner than men, but Anna Vyrubova more than most. Since the age of seventeen she had adored Alexandra, grateful to her for visiting her in her illness, and thereafter she had become the Empress's tool. Alexandra had even arranged what she considered to be a suitable marriage for her. He recalled how only recently Anna had revealed the unhappy affair to him.

"His name was Boris Vyrubov, and he was very handsome, but—I think his nerves had been shattered at the battle of Tsushima, for he could be very odd at times." Anna's face had flushed at such an admission, but she went on.

"All went comparatively well for a couple of months, and then he had to go away. The Tsarina came to visit me, and while she was there Boris came home. I believe his ship had engine trouble, so he was to be delayed for a few days. But the Empress would not let him come in; her guards were surrounding the house, and he grew angry. After she had gone, he forced his way in, screaming abuse at me. It was obvious he was jealous of our friendship, the Empress said. Anyway, he—he attacked me. Very brutally. I fled to the Tsarina's palace and she took me in. She arranged the divorce. So, you see, I have reason to be grateful to her."

Rasputin refrained from pointing out to her that her dilemma had been due to the Empress in the first place. The fact was that Anna now lived in the palace, constantly at Alexandra's side, and her influence on his behalf could be enormous. Whatever rumours might reach the Empress about his womanising and debauchery, Anna would firmly deny them, reminding Alexandra that he was a holy man with many miracles to his credit.

His arm was becoming cramped. Rasputin pushed the girl's head off. She woke and looked up at him dreamily.

"Again?" she asked.

"No, I want more wine. My throat is parched in this heat."

The scent of limes hung heavy over the tents and booths up on the hill, and the fires flickered an orange light into the darkening sky. Gypsy songs borne on the breeze grew louder and more frenzied, and Rasputin could hear the hand-clapping that no doubt accompanied the movements of a dusky-limbed dancer in the firelight.

"Go, fetch me some more of that delicious red, cool Caucasian wine," he said, giving her a push. The girl rose reluctantly. "And hurry back. When I have drunk my fill, I shall mount you again, my pretty sow. Hurry!"

She moved away, her long-limbed, graceful walk giving him pleasure, but as she neared the tents Rasputin heard the sound of singing die away, a horse's hooves canter to a halt, and a sharp voice calling out.

"In the name of the Tsar!" it cried imperiously. "In the name of the Tsar I demand to know if one Gregory Efimovitch Rasputin is among you!"

Rasputin heard the demand clearly on the now still night air. He rose leisurely and walked uphill to join the gypsies by the fire. A small, stocky man with a moustache stood impatiently fingering his riding crop. "Well?" he demanded at length. The gypsies stood silent.

"I am he," Rasputin said quietly. All the faces turned to watch him curiously, and the little man's registered relief.

"The Lord be praised! I have searched all over St Petersburg for you tonight."

"Then your mission must be urgent."

99

The little man wiped the sweat from his brow. "Indeed it is, starets. Come aside." Out of earshot of the curious bystanders the man caught Rasputin's sleeve. "You must go to the Winter Palace with all haste, Father, for the Empress is in despair."

"What ails her, man? I am relaxing from my labours with my friends. Must I be disturbed even now?" He did not feel the irritation that his words implied; only pleasure that the tsarina should turn to him. His power grew by the minute. He felt his whole body begin to glow with a suffused warmth, and he stared ahead into the darkness, as if he could see what the power would bring.

"Waste no more time, I beg you, starets," the little man said, gazing up at him beseechingly. "Her Majesty bade me find you and bring you with all speed. It seems the little Tsarevitch is ill, dangerously ill, and she says no one but you can save him now the doctors have given him up. For God's sake, come quickly! Take my horse if you will, and I'll follow."

Rasputin did not move for a moment, but stood as motionless as if frozen. Then he sank to his knees on the grass, unaware of the gypsies grouped about the fire, and covered his face with his hands. The little man hovered uncertainly, still clutching the reins of his horse.

Rasputin's shoulders shook, his great body trembling, and the gypsies fell silent. Then after a moment he rose, his eyes gleaming triumphantly, and he raised his left arm as if in salute.

"Hear me!" he cried aloud, his great coarse voice echoing over the silent hill. "The Tsarevitch was dying! I have prayed for him. The crisis is already past, and he will recover."

He swung himself up on the horse's back and turned, motioned the man to climb up behind him, and rode off. Not a murmur rippled through the crowd of watching gypsies until he had completely disappeared from sight.

Entering the Tsar's Winter Palace by a side door, Rasputin was led straight up to the little prince's nursery. The Empress rushed to his side and, regardless of his dirty linen shirt and coarse, matted hair, she clung to his arm tightly.

"Help me, friend! If ever I needed help, it is now!" Her voice came in a strangled sob, and her eyes were wide and staring in defeat. Rasputin released her fingers from his sleeve and spoke harshly.

"Matushka, I have prayed for the Tsarevitch half an hour ago. He will not die. From that moment on his condition improved."

She stared at him uncomprehendingly. "He will recover, I tell you," Rasputin went on.

"Is it true? Is it possible?" Her voice was no more than a murmur. "I have been in the chapel praying. Let us go to him."

"You will see," Rasputin said as they walked. "And he will live as long as I am here to watch over him, Matushka."

Alexandra moved through the crowd of nurses and doctors about the cot and bent over it, feeling the little forehead and listening.

"It is true," she breathed at last. "He breathes more easily and he is not so hot now." She turned to Rasputin, a radiant smile lighting up her weary face. "Oh, my friend, you are indeed God's mediator! You must never leave me, promise you will not. You have saved my son's life and for that I can never thank you enough."

She took his big, coarse hand in hers and covered it with kisses, unaware of the malevolent glances exchanged between the doctors. Botkin and Fedorov began to speak of the Tsarevitch's unexpected improvement, but she cut them short.

"I know and I thank God for it. And especially we must thank our dear friend Rasputin for his intervention on our behalf. Once again you have proved your miracle-working. Rasputin, irrefutably. I shall be for ever in your debt."

She left the room then with Rasputin, content that her precious son would sleep peacefully tonight, no longer at death's door nor tormented by agony. Rasputin stopped at the door.

"I shall stay and pray by him all night," he announced.

"You are too good," the Empress sighed. "Then Nicky and I shall do likewise."

That night everyone was sent from the room but the Tsar and Tsarina and the holy man. Rasputin knelt all night at the cotside, but Nicholas and Alexandra fell asleep in their chairs, exhausted from three nights of staying anxiously awake. Alexandra awoke suddenly. It was nearing dawn. Candles burned only before the ikons, and in their soft glow she saw Rasputin's bowed head beside her sleeping son. She tiptoed to the cot. The boy looked better already, and relief flooded her aching body.

Rasputin looked up, his grey eyes penetrating and brilliant in the candlelight. Alexandra whispered across the cot.

"God bless you, Rasputin. God bless you."

Rasputin looked at her for a moment, then spoke tonelessly. "He will live, Matushka, as I told you, as long as I am here."

FOURTEEN

THE sun was high in the St Petersburg sky by the time Rasputin walked home from the palace to his two-storeyed house in the Nevsky Prospect the next day. His heart was jubilant and he had to exercise great control not to execute great leaps of joy as he walked. He had been sent for to the Imperial Palace, and as a result of the night's doings the door of the palace would be for ever open to him from now on. He had good reason to be proud of himself.

It was only as he turned into his house that he noticed the two silent figures cross over the street and stand facing the house, taking out notebooks as they did so. Of course, the Ochrana—the secret police. His movements would be of even greater significance to them now that he was free to enter the Imperial Palace. He could expect to see them as his constant shadows from now on.

A neighbour leaned out of a window as Rasputin approached the door, but he withdrew without speaking. No doubt he believed Rasputin to be coming home from yet another night's drunken orgy, and Rasputin was tempted to shout aloud, so that the whole Prospect might hear, that it was no orgy but the conquest of the Empress herself that he had just completed. She was so transparently impressed by him, so utterly convinced that he was a saint in disguise, that Rasputin could have roared with laughter. Women were always gullible and impressionable, but this neurotic Empress was the easiest of them all. And through her, the Tsar would become a tractable creature too, for it was obvious how much he doted on her. If she truly felt the starets Rasputin was indispensable to her son's health and she believed in his sanctity, then the Tsar would make him as welcome at the Winter Palace as the Tsarina herself.

Rasputin mounted the stairs, his heart alight with joy and a sense of achievement. It was true he was tired now after his night's vigil, but his spirits were soaring. A group of people clustered about the door straightened as he approached. Their pale, earnest faces brightened at the sight of him.

An elderly man was the first to speak. "If it is not too much trouble to you, starets . . ."

"Here, I was first!" a plump peasant woman cut in, elbowing him out of the way. "I was here at first light!"

Rasputin passed them as if he had not heard. The voices faded away and the pale faces waited. He raised his hand slowly in salute, and the irritable look left them. He gazed at each face slowly in turn, all but the peasant wench in a kerchief who kept her head bowed. They looked back at him hopefully, a mixture of anticipation and awe on their grey faces. Rasputin savoured the feeling of power over them that it bred in him.

"I can see none of you today," he said at last curtly, and heard the murmurs of disappointment as he went into his room. Before he closed the door he waited to watch their reaction to his next statement. "I have been all night at the bedside of the Tsarevitch, and I am tired."

Again the look of awe and respect leapt into the grey faces, and some crossed themselves in pious admiration. The peasant girl looked up. It was Tanya.

"You may go. Perhaps I shall see some of you tomorrow," Rasputin said finally, but he beckoned to the girl. The others began to shamble away, muttering amongst themselves and he could hear snatches of "Tsarevitch's bedside" and "at the Winter Palace". Now they were indelibly impressed.

Tanya waited until they had all gone and then came forward timidly. He realised he had seen very little of her since that Bloody Sunday two years ago when she had lost her husband. But since she had also lost the hollow, defeated look she wore then, he could only assume that life treated her better nowadays. He took her hands in his.

"How is it with you, Tanya? Did you also come to seek my help?"

"No, Gregory. I came only to thank you for helping me when I was alone and friendless in a strange city. All goes well with me now, dear friend, and it is to you I owe my gratitude."

She looked well too, her cheeks plump and rosy despite the lack of provisions in the city. And she wore an air of contentment and poise that betokened security. She was a very attractive young woman. A well-known flicker ran through Rasputin's veins, exploding into an inferno of desire for a lissom woman, and the fatigue and denial of his night's vigil served only to strengthen the yearning. His hands trembled, on the verge of seizing her and carrying her to the bedroom, but the wide-eyed innocence of her gaze unmanned him.

Devil take him, what was wrong with him? he fumed inwardly. Hadn't he taken a score of women with even more seeming innocence than her, disguising his lust with a thin veil of saintly well-meaning? And had they not all, without exception, swallowed the excuse? Having robbed so many maidens of their virginity, high and low born, why hesitate over Tanya?

But his reasoning could not prevail. Tanya was no virgin, he argued further, but still the clear dark eyes gazed at him reverently and robbed him of the power to touch her. Instead he spoke to her gently, letting go of her hands.

"Have you married again, Tanya?"

She blushed and lowered her gaze. "No, but I am keeping company with a Cossack from the palace. Ivan he is named, and I think perhaps one day he will ask me to marry him."

Rasputin turned away, yawning and making no attempt to cover his gaping mouth. Tanya jumped with dismayed concern.

"Oh, I am sorry, Gregory! In my happiness I forget your fatigue! I shall leave you to sleep now—and may the blessing of God be always with you, my dear friend. I am proud to have known you, and shall bless you always as a saint."

And she was gone. Next day Rasputin did not see the suppliants who came to his door in search of him, for a closed carriage came to fetch him to Tsarskoe Selo. Rasputin grinned broadly, all trace of weariness gone. It was a high tribute to the Empress's need of him that she sent for him royally. He rode in state the few miles out of the city, looking out at the palace's terraces and statues with pride. He passed through its polished halls, its marble statuary and crystal chandeliers, its velvet and silks and Oriental rugs and scent-laden air, smiling with pleasure to see the myriad silent servants and lackeys who bowed and backed deferentially. This was the life he had been destined for, respected and revered by even the highest in the land. Pokrovskoe and his gentle wife Praskovie seemed an eternity away.

And thus it was every day now. The carriage came to fetch him, the Empress welcomed him warmly as her dear friend, the starets, and clung to his arm as she took him to see the children. The Tsarevitch grew stronger daily and the Empress shed a tear each time she renewed her thanks to the holy man.

In the next few weeks there was a distinct change in

Rasputin, in appearance at least. The Empress greeted him one afternoon with a heavily embroidered silk shirt.

"For you, starets, if you will do me the honour to accept it. I embroidered it myself, and every stitch contains a loving thought for you," she said shyly as she offered him the gift.

And on succeeding days he found gaily coloured tunics awaiting him or velvet breeches or a pair of soft leather boots. He accepted them all with pleasure. After all, if he were to move constantly among the richest and noblest in the land, they would have no cause to sneer at him behind their perfumed hands. Each day he changed one vivid silk shirt for another, and belted it round with a silken cord with a dangling tassel. He trimmed his shaggy beard and lank hair, and fastened Alexandra's handsome gift of a gold cross on a chain about his neck.

He chuckled as he entered fine boyar salons thus attired. He might be but a common Siberian peasant, attributed with saintliness, but he was human enough to revel in his splendid new luxury. He was as good as any of the St Petersburg nobles now, and treated them as familiarly as his status warranted.

Like Olga, for instance. The Grand Duchess Olga Alexandrovna, sister of the Tsar, had been sitting with the Empress one afternoon in the Empress's mauve boudoir when he arrived. She had eyed him curiously for a time, and obviously had not welcomed the grip of his horny, calloused hands on hers. Nor had her eyes softened when he began to ply her with questions.

"Are you happy, Olga?" he had begun, and then, "Do you love your husband?" She had flushed with embarrassment and made some kind of social noise, and Rasputin demanded, "Then why have you no children?" It amused him to see her discomfort, and how the Empress looked away uncomfortably.

In her eyes at least he could do no wrong. He pressed his advantage as often as he could.

"I need a thousand roubles for a man who is in debt," he would tell Alexandra with a cool, calculating stare. "Will you give it to me, Matushka?"

And invariably she did. What a pity he was not a self-seeking man, Rasputin thought, or he could become immensely wealthy through this weak, neurotic woman. But he was not. He kept only what money he needed for himself for drinking and whoring and to send to Praskovie, and he gave the rest away.

More and more people sought him out now, not only the poor and the sick in need of help, but the nobles too who considered it an honour to welcome into their homes someone so eminent and persona grata with the Royal Family. Rasputin accepted all their invitations cheerfully, dining at their elegant tables as if he were still in Pokrovskoe, plunging his hands into the soup and wiping them dry on the fine linen tablecloth. It gave him immense satisfaction to parade his lowly origins, to talk of the swine and their sex life in his native village, to enlarge upon the details with expressive gestures and to watch the company's looks of disgust weakly change to polite smiles. He had them in the palm of his hand, to do with as he would, and Rasputin luxuriated in the feeling of power.

Daily those impressed by his strength and power and hypnotic eyes came to seek him out. He gave tea parties, mostly attended by women, the wives of nobles and officers who had been fascinated by his sensual, animal appeal. Rasputin responded as they hoped. The talk around the tea table was lewd and suggestive, and no one demurred when he led one of the women at a time into his bedroom.

"He is indeed a saint!" a maid would cry out in ecstasy after leaving his bedroom. "Such a communion is indeed holy and blessed!" Women, of whatever class, revelled in his rough, exciting love-making, and believed themselves the better for having experienced it. Rasputin pronounced his dogma earnestly.

"There is no salvation but through sin and redemption," he told his ardent followers. "I am the voice of God. Intercourse with me cannot be a sin."

They accepted his words joyfully, revelling in their abandonment and the thrilling fulfilment of their desires. When he had done, and many women had received his sensual communion, Rasputin blessed them all with the sign of the cross and bade them depart. And with pure consciences they left, glowing with happiness.

Rasputin was immeasurably proud of his success and power in the capital. He was still a fairly regular visitor to the palace, and it pleased him to see the Empress's tearful face on occasion when she reproached him.

"You have not been to see us lately, starets. The children have been asking for you. We miss you when you are absent overlong."

Rasputin would remind her then of his holy duties which he could not ignore, and the Empress would agree reluctantly. Even Tsar Nicholas greeted him like a long-lost friend.

"Alexandra has missed you so, dear friend. She needs your strength and comfort. Do come to us more often. Our doors are ever open to you."

But Rasputin spent more and more time at his own house with his ardent devotees, purifying the God-seeking women who sought his embrace to attain holiness. It was a labour of love, and he enjoyed it. Still the Ochrana watched his every move to the palace, to the brothels and to the gypsy camp, but Rasputin did not care. In the confidence of the Tsar and the Empress, he was unimpeachable. But after a couple of years of giddy power, Rasputin began to feel an uneasy sense that something was wrong. He would have to act quickly if he were to consolidate his power before it waned.

FIFTEEN

Rasputin lay in bed puzzling, trying to sift out the niggling thought that was worrying him. He had no tangible evidence to prove he was slipping, just a vague sense of unease. It was a fact that one who enjoyed the confidence of the Tsar and the Empress, who had open access to them when very few others did, was bound to be unpopular in certain quarters, to have enemies even amongst the politicians.

But he had done no harm to anyone through his power, had he? He had secured a few minor appointments for the sons of suppliants who came to his door, but where was the harm in that?

Perhaps he was envied by the Court circle, the churchmen and ministers about the Tsar who never knew which way their vacillating monarch would turn, because he knew Nicholas's every thought. They could not rely on the Tsar's word, knowing he might change his mind at any moment, but Rasputin knew Nicholas always followed every word of advice Rasputin offered. Even the Ministry of the Interior were obliged to bribe Prince Andronikov to keep them informed of the Tsar's moves, not because Andronikov enjoyed Nicholas's confidence, but because the prince was a well-known homosexual whose chief lover was the groom of the Tsar's bedchamber.

Rasputin smiled bitterly. The most these envious men could hope for was to learn of the Tsar's plans, while he himself was in a position to influence them. He wondered at his own naïvety, that he had not suspected their jealousy earlier. Though Rasputin neither knew nor cared much about politics, these men must indeed bear him a grudge. He must watch his step carefully if he was not to let them undo him.

It was almost unnoticeable at first, but gradually Rasputin came to realise that his popularity was not so great as it had been over the past few years. In minor incidents at first it appeared.

There had been the pretty serving-maid at the palace who had caught his eye as he was leaving one evening. She had lowered her eyes decorously at his suggestive murmurs, but he had caught a glimpse of the amused anticipation in her eyes.

"In here," he had urged, drawing her into an empty ante-room, and within minutes he had shown her how energetic a Siberian stallion could be. She had smiled happily before he left, but the following day the Empress had taken him to task.

"One of the maids says you raped her, starets. Can I believe it?" she had asked, her eyes round with obvious disbelief. It had taken many soothing words and an admission from the girl herself that she had been willing, to soothe the fluttered Empress. Rasputin reflected sadly that not to long ago Alexandra would not even have questioned him on the matter, flatly refusing to listen to a word against her dear friend.

Then there was the evening when he dined at Anna Vyrubova's house with the Grand Duchess Olga and the Tsar and Tsarina. For some strange reason, when Anna went to see the royal couple off, he had had the oddest desire to make love to Olga, the Tsar's sister, just to prove his mastery. But no sooner had he put his arm about her and begun to caress her than she sprang to her feet and left the room. It was a stupid overture on his part, for now she refused to admit him to her palace. He had even had Anna intercede for him, but Olga was adamant. It was the beginning of the faint rumblings that disturbed him.

Not very long afterwards he went to Tsarskoe Selo in the evening. The Empress was delighted.

"The children are going to bed," she said. "Would you like to see them before they retire?"

"I shall say prayers with the Tsarevitch," Rasputin replied, and went upstairs. The four princesses were laughingly playing with their little brother, all of them in their nightclothes. After prayers were over, Rasputin lingered to watch the girls. They were very pretty, and Olga and Tatiana already showed the lush, full-bosomed beauty of their mother. He could not resist a few lascivious thoughts, and did not notice their governess, Mademoiselle Tiutcheva, staring at him in horrified disgust.

She had obviously spoken of her fears to the Empress, because Alexandra took Rasputin aside on his next visit.

"Mlle Tiutcheva was concerned about your being with the girls in their nightclothes," she said timidly, her pretty face pink with embarrassment. "She demanded that you be barred from the nursery henceforth."

Rasputin stared at her in disbelief. "And what will you do, Matushka? Will you be ordered by a servant?"

"No, no, of course not. I have dismissed her for such wicked thoughts and she will return to Moscow immediately. But Nicholas . . ."

"What does Batiushka say?"

"He says it is not seemly for a man to be with such grown girls, and begs you will avoid the nursery at night."

Alexandra's wide blue eyes were full of apology, but the words were spoken nonetheless. And they began a ripple. In Moscow, Tiutcheva spread the story which reached the ears of the Empress's sister, the Grand Duchess Elizabeth, who was a religious fanatic. What she said of Rasputin to her sister he could only guess, but it was certain to be highly unpleasant and could only serve to weaken his position yet again. The frown between Rasputin's eyes deepened.

But life was for living and Rasputin was ever the optimist. He continued his life much as before, drinking and whoring and seducing the women who sought him out. Only when he found the doors of his patron, the Grand Duchess Militsa, closed against him did the vexing thought arise again.

"Nor will the Grand Duchess Stana receive you," he was told by a lackey at Militsa's door.

"But the Grand Duke Nicholas—he has reason to be grateful to me," Rasputin protested, recalling the incident of the dog.

"Not any more, starets. He has said he wishes never to see the devil again." The door was closed firmly in Rasputin's face.

And when his close Church friends, the Bishops Theophan and Hermogen, received him coolly, Rasputin began really to fret. He was unprepared, however, for the Empress's accusation.

"Rasputin, the Bishop Theophan has laid a serious charge against you, of seducing women lasciviously in the name of religion. What have you to say?"

Her voice was decidedly cooler than he had ever heard before. He feigned surprise and ignorance of the charge. How should Theophan know anyway?

"Because these women confessed their sins to him, including the sin of fornication with you." The Empress turned aside coldly, ignoring the friendly hand he placed on her shoulder. Rasputin's wits worked furiously.

"I should like to talk to Batiushka about the charge against me," he said quietly. "It is not true and I am surprised that Theophan should malign me so."

"Very well."

114

Alexandra left him alone to speak with Nicholas, and Rasputin was heartened to find that the Tsar did not regard the charge as a very serious one. Nevertheless, Rasputin urged him to remove Theophan. He was hardly a suitable man to direct the Theological Academy if he could speak such perfidy against a fellow holy man. Nicholas listened, wavered and finally agreed. Theophan was transferred to become Bishop of the Crimea.

"Now I have shut his trap!" Rasputin gloated as he walked home triumphantly, but his triumph was short-lived. And the bitterness was increased because it was an erstwhile friend who now denounced him, the monk Iliodor, whom he thought he could trust.

Iliodor was an earnest young zealot, given to preaching fiery sermons. He believed in the equality of all men under the autocratic rule of the Tsar, and Rasputin had believed he could be a useful ally.

"Then come and visit my monastery at Tsaritsyn," Iliodor had responded proudly. "We built it by hand ourselves."

"Gladly, my friend," Rasputin had replied. He had enjoyed the stay at Tsaritsyn, for the fervent parishioners had included many pretty young girls, and he had seduced and purified them abundantly. Iliodor had said nothing. Then they travelled on to Pokrovskoe together, and in the joy of being acclaimed by his wife and family and all the admiring villagers, Rasputin had swelled with pride.

"I am supreme in my power," he told Iliodor. "No women ever resist me, not even the Empress herself can remain deaf to my words." He enjoyed the puzzled look that crossed Iliodor's face, for he had chosen his words carefully to have an ambiguous meaning.

"It is true," he went on boastfully. "I have kissed her in her children's nursery before now. Why, even the Tsar believes me infallible. Do you know what he said to me? He said, 'Gregory, you are the very Christ.' That's what he said. He cannot breathe without me, nor make any decision."

That had been foolish of him of course, Rasputin realised now, but Iliodor had kept silent and not repeated what he heard to the bishops—not then, anyway. But what had been even more foolish was to prove his mastery over Iliodor by succeeding where he failed. That show of braggartism had alienated Iliodor's friendship for ever. One occasion was at Tsaritsyn, when a young carter came knocking at the door.

"For the love of heaven, I beg you to come," he besought Iliodor. "My wife has been attacked by the devil! I think she is possessed!"

Iliodor snatched up a bottle of holy water and followed his parishioner to his cottage, with Rasputin hard on his heels. A young peasant woman lay writhing on the floor, her hands clutching her head and her eyes staring. Slaver trickled from the corners of her lips as she screamed.

The young husband put his fingers in his eyes to try and shut out the obscenities she shrieked, and crossed himself fervently as Iliodor opened the bottle and sprinkled her writhing body with the water, murmuring incantations as he did so. The girl went on twisting and blaspheming. Iliodor exorcised the spirit, but still it would not leave. Rasputin watched in silence. Minutes passed, but the girl's condition remained the same. At last Iliodor stopped and looked up at him helplessly.

"Will you leave me alone with her for five minutes?" Rasputin asked quietly. Iliodor hesitated, then nodded. The young carter followed him out unquestioningly.

But a full half-hour elapsed before Rasputin led the girl out by the hand. She was quiet now and gazing at him with huge, black eyes.

"I have driven out the devil," Rasputin said quietly, and neither the husband nor Iliodor had asked how. And then again, a few days later, he had revived Madame Lebedev's niece from a deep coma after all Iliodor's attempts had failed. Yes, on reflection Rasputin realised he had not acted wisely where Iliodor was concerned.

But when Rasputin's eye was attracted by a pretty little nun he spotted in the Prospect one evening, he little realised he was now about to provoke Iliodor's unleashed rage.

"No, please," the little nun said as his hands glided under her habit, but her eyes had invited where her words had not. Rasputin played the reluctant fish with more patience than was his wont, but in the end she refused.

"No, certainly not, starets. It is sinful," she said with a show of hurt dignity and innocence. Rasputin's lust and anger both rose to floodtide simultaneously, and he threw her down unceremoniously and took her without further ado.

She fled, screaming and bleeding and bent on revenge. Iliodor's pent-up anger burst forth, and he confronted Rasputin with Bishop Hermogen.

Rasputin shiftly uneasily before the bishop's glaring gaze. It was embarrassing to have witnesses—Iliodor, a Cossack, a journalist, and the idiot Mitya who used to be the Court prophet until Rasputin ousted him. His account of what took place today, and the journalist's report in the St Petersburg press, would ruin Rasputin's career completely if he did not make a good showing. He glanced back at the bishop contemptuously.

"Is it true, what I hear?" the bishop asked at length. "Your sexual orgies—the nun—is it indeed true?"

"Every word." Rasputin spoke the words proudly, tossing his long mane defiantly.

"Dear God!" the bishop moaned, his back to Rasputin.

Then suddenly he turned, snatched up a heavy wooden cross that stood on the table between them, and began belabouring Rasputin soundly over the head with it.

"You cheat, you fraud!" the bishop bellowed in a most ungodly manner. "As you have destroyed, so should you be destroyed!"

Rasputin dodged and covered his head against the rain of blows, but the elderly bishop was too enraged to be defeated thus easily. Iliodor stood and watched in satisfaction.

"Leave me be!" Rasputin cried out, "or I shall make short work of you!"

"Do you dare to threaten me?" the bishop roared. "I shall deal with you for once and all. Fetch me that ikon." The Cossack hastened forward with it. Hermogen pushed it before Rasputin's face, the wooden cross upraised in his other hand.

"Now—will you swear to abjure women, and to leave the Tsar's family in peace?"

Rasputin hesitated and glanced up fearfully at the cross. He was in no position to argue, with three others standing by to help the bishop if need be.

"Well? Will you swear?"

"I'll swear. Yes, yes, of course I will." And he did swear, loudly and enthusiastically, to leave women and the Royal Family alone. It was a very abject Rasputin who crawled home to his house that day, and an even more deflated one who begged to see Hermogen the next day to explain and atone.

"Certainly not," said the servant at the door. "His Grace says he will never see you again—never and nowhere."

Very well, thought Rasputin. If he wants open warfare, so let it be. And he went as quickly as possible to Tsarskoe Selo to see Tsar Nicholas.

SIXTEEN

Tsar Nicholas paced the length of his book-lined study angrily. Rasputin stood watching to see the effect of his words. His head and shoulders had more or less recovered from his beating now, though the bruises still remained.

"Can this be true?" the Tsar muttered. "Even a bishop cannot escape the punishment for laying hands on a starets. He must be banished, to a distant monastery where he can do no more harm. I will not have my authority flouted."

Rasputin bowed his head meekly, but inwardly he delighted at his victory over Hermogen. "And what of Iliodor?" he ventured.

"He did not beat you. I shall consider the matter."

"But he did rape Madame Loktin, an officer's wife, and then pretended she had tried to seduce him. She had to suffer the punishment of being stripped and beaten and tied to the back of a cart and dragged through the snow because of his lies. He is a wicked man." Not a flicker of guilt troubled Rasputin as he spoke. Iliodor was a powerful enemy and must be removed.

"Very well. He too must be banished, but to a different monastery," the Tsar pronounced after a pause. Rasputin left the palace, highly satisfied with his revenge.

But the affair was not yet over. Iliodor refused to go quietly into banishment. He roamed the country denouncing Rasputin and his evil influence at Court, and declared that the wicked starets had even put a spell on the Empress. To prove his point he produced letters from Alexandra to Rasputin, made copies of them and circulated them widely. The first Rasputin came to hear of them was when he visited the Empress one afternoon in her mauve boudoir. She was lying, as usual, on her couch in a flowing négligée and in her hand she held a piece of paper. She was pale as she handed it to him.

"Do you remember this, dear friend?"

Rasputin took the printed sheet and began to read.

"My beloved, unforgettable teacher, redeemer and mentor! How tiresome it is without you! My soul is quiet and I relax only when you, my teacher, are sitting beside me. I kiss your hands and lean my head on your blessed shoulder. Oh, how light, how light do I feel then! I only wish one thing—to fall asleep forever on your shoulders and in your arms. What happiness to feel your presence near me! Where are you? Where have you gone? Oh, I am so sad and my heart is longing. . . . Will you soon be again close to me? Come quickly, I am waiting for you and I am tormenting myself for you. I am asking for your holy blessing and I am kissing your blessed hands. I love you forever.   Yours, M."

Rasputin coughed and cleared his throat. He remembered it well—a letter from her to him some two years ago. M for Matushka, the name he called her by. And he also remembered that the letter had disappeared from his possession while he was travelling with Iliodor.

"Someone is spreading malicious rumours about us, Gregory, and using this as evidence," Alexandra said quietly, not looking him in the face.

"Rubbish!" Rasputin exploded. "You always write in this vein, to Anna, to me, to everyone!" He could have said more —that the emotional writings of a highly-strung woman were open to misinterpretation, but he did not want to offend her by suggesting that she was too openly emotional. Blast Iliodor! He was still making trouble, even from a distance.

So it was satisfying to learn shortly afterwards that the Holy

Synod, wholly disapproving of Iliodor's mischief and offended by his suggestion that they were bowing down to the Devil, had unfrocked the rebel priest. What Rasputin did not know then was that Iliodor, enraged and frustrated, then set vigorously about forming an organisation whose sole aim was to wreak vengeance on Rasputin. If he had known, it would no doubt have tickled his broad sense of humour to hear the ironic justice they planned.

"My children, listen to me," Iliodor was urging a group of women and girls who had all been ill-used by Rasputin at one time or another. "Shall such a monster as he be allowed to go on living and destroying?"

"No, no!" they cried in unison.

"Then what shall we do with him?"

"Castrate him! Destroy him as he has us!"

"So let it be!" Iliodor roared in pleasure. "Take your opportunity, whenever it may occur. Carry a knife for the purpose wherever you go. And if the chance comes—slash—and be sure you reach your mark!"

"Into the black devil's heart," one girl shrieked. "Death is too good for the beast! He must die for his evil deeds!"

Iliodor's eyes gleamed. "Come forward, girl. What is your name?"

"Khina Guseva, Father."

"And what has Rasputin done that you should hate him so?"

The girl's eyes gleamed with malice. "He used me, as he has done countless others, and then he cast me aside like a filthy, worn-out shoe. If ever I lay eyes on him again, I swear I'll do him in, before God I swear it!"

Iliodor murmured and considered a moment. Then he picked up a knife, threaded a cord through a hole in its handle, and bade her unfasten her blouse. She did so without a word, and Iliodor tied the cord about her neck. The knife lay, long and sharp and gleaming, against the bronzed skin of her breast.

"When the chance comes, use this knife to kill Rasputin," he said quietly. "I shall no longer be here, but I shall wait far away and listen for the good news that he is dead."

"You will hear it," Khina assured him. "I promise you that, Father. You will hear."

But Rasputin knew nothing of the plot to castrate or kill him. All he learned was that a few months later the troublesome Iliodor had disguised himself as a woman and slipped unperceived across the frontier into Finland, and he breathed a sigh of relief.

But still Rasputin was not happy. Since the Tsarevitch's illness in 1907 he had wielded great power in the capital for four years, but after the recent rumblings against him it was apparent the Tsar and Tsarina did not welcome him to the palace so warmly as before. Not that they respected and loved him any less, but simply because they considered it more discreet, they told him with concern.

"Even in the palace the secret police watch and report on everything that passes," Alexandra told him sadly. "We consider it safer to behave with circumspection, for your sake as well as ours."

He knew she meant it truly when she told him they loved him just as dearly as before, for he had told her often enough that her young son's continued prosperity depended on his being close by. Word came to his ears through Anna Vyrubova, the woman closest to the Empress, that Dr Botkin, the Tsarevitch's physician, who had always been jealous of the Empress's regard for Rasputin, tried to warn Alexandra that her dear friend was reviled and hated by St Petersburg society because of his cunning. She firmly refused to hear ill of him,

Rasputin was glad to learn, telling Botkin, "Saints are always calumniated. He is hated because we love him."

All St Petersburg society followed Militsa's example in closing their doors to him, and he had only actresses and whores and gypsy girls to turn to for consolation.

At least he was still secure in the Royal Family's esteem then, Rasputin consoled himself, despite his waning popularity in the city.

But he had not bargained for Stolypin, the Tsar's able and energetic Prime Minister. Since Stolypin took over five years ago Russia's prosperity had increased, her crops had flourished and the railways and foreign investments had made her economy stronger than ever before. But Stolypin had always resented Rasputin's influence with the Tsar, which always worked against the advice of the Duma. He now, without recourse to the Tsar, ordered an investigation into Rasputin's affairs and presented his report to Nicholas.

Nicholas read it and put it away. He was not prepared to take notice of it or act upon it. A few days later Alexandra burst into his study where Nicholas sat at his desk, wearing his peasant uniform and smoking. He looked up at her unexpected intrusion.

"What is it, my dear? Why do you look so agitated?" His heart skipped a beat. "It's not Alexis, is it?"

"No, no, the boy is well. But Stolypin has ordered Rasputin into exile! He is to leave St Petersburg at once!"

"How do you know?"

"Gregory is in my boudoir. He asked me to countermand the order, or to ask you to do so. You will, will you not, Nicky? I cannot let him go!"

"I cannot overrule my Prime Minister, Alex."

"But you can! You are the Tsar! Nicky, we need him! Alexi's life depends upon him!"

"Stolypin knows what benefit the boy derives from Gregory, for he has seen him with his own eyes bring relief to the child's pain. If he deems it wiser for Rasputin to leave the capital, then he probably has good reason."

Alexandra turned pale. "You do not believe the slanderous reports about Gregory and me, surely?"

"Certainly not!" Nicholas rose and took hold of his wife's shoulders. "No, my dear, I know our love is only for each other. But Stolypin has proved right so often in the past, I would not want to countermand him now. Gregory may travel for a time and then return to us."

"But if Alexis should need him . . ." the Tsarina cried. "Oh, Nicholas, I am afraid! I still sense the evil that is to befall our family!"

But Nicholas refused to act against Stolypin's order of banishment. Alexandra wept and begged in vain.

"I hate him!" she cried at last. "I hate Stolypin because he severs my child from his very life blood! He will pay for this, I know it. He will regret this day!"

She did not have to wait long to see retribution overcome the Prime Minister. Rasputin left the capital at once, first to visit Pokrovskoe and then to begin a pilgrimage to Jerusalem. By the autumn of 1911 he had reached Kiev, and, as luck would have it, the Tsar came to Kiev to unveil a statue of his father.

Rasputin stood silent and unnoticed in the vast crowd and watched the procession of carriages clatter past. Nicholas looked ahead, pale and erect, his coach surrounded by guards and police, and in another carriage behind him sat Stolypin and another minister, Kokovtsov. Rasputin stared hard at Stolypin, who was quite unaware of his presence, and as he did so a strange feeling came over him. It was that odd sensation of startling clarity, of pellucid perception, that had occurred often since that time as a child when he had known the peasant horse-stealer in Pokrovskoe.

It was there, undeniably there, a huge black intangible cloud hovering over Stolypin's head and about to engulf him. Rasputin shuddered and began to mumble involuntarily. People about him turned to look at him curiously. He could not help it. The mumbles in his throat grew into a huge roar, and he cried out at the top of his voice, revealing the terrible vision that was so clear to his inner sight and so inevitable.

"Death! Death is after him! Death is driving behind Stolypin!"

SEVENTEEN

IT WAS on the very next day that the assassin's bullet found its mark in Stolypin's heart. The Kiev Opera House was packed for the performance of "Tsar Sultan" because the imperial party was to attend. Kiev citizens gazed with awe at Tsar Nicholas sitting in a box with his daughters Olga and Tatiana, overlooking the front row where Stolypin sat with other officials. The Opera House was hot and airless.

During the second interval Nicholas and the Grand Duchesses left the box to breathe the cooler air outside. Stolypin rose and stretched himself. At the same moment a young man in evening dress walked quickly down the aisle towards him, drew a revolver, and fired twice. Stolypin fell forward.

Women began to scream as officials pounced on the young man. Stolypin, clutching the seat back, made the sign of the Cross in the air and slowly sank to the ground. No one noticed the Tsar and his daughters re-enter their box and stand fascinated with horror at the sight below them. Stolypin's jacket was unbuttoned to show the rapidly-spreading crimson stain on his chest.

Enraged bystanders would have lynched the young man, and, in fact, before the police could drag him away to a private room two of his teeth had been knocked out. The orchestra played the national anthem and the atmosphere grew calmer once he was gone, but tongues speculated all night as to why Stolypin had been attacked, and not the Tsar.

126

Rasputin learnt of the shooting some days after, and by then Stolypin had died after five days of clinging to life.

"I knew it, I knew it," Rasputin murmured to himself. "I could see death hovering over him so clearly."

The assassin, a revolutionary named Mordka Bogrov, was caught and hanged, and Tsar Nicholas appointed a new Prime Minister, Kokovtsov. Rasputin continued on his journey to the Holy Land. But during his journey he wrote constantly to the Empress, and received rapturous letters from her.

On his return he settled for a time in Pokrovskoe. Praskovie accepted her husband's return with the loving resignation that she always did.

"But how long will it be before you go away again?" she asked him once.

"When the Empress sends for me, as she will." He spent the time enjoying the children he hardly knew—Maria was now sixteen, Dimitri thirteen and Varvara eleven. From what he heard of events in St Petersburg it seemed advantageous to stay where he was for the time being. Censorship now having been lifted from the press, scurrilous attacks were being mounted against him and his power over the Tsar and Tsarina. Reports were printed of confessions from his victims, the women he had raped or seduced, and outraged mothers called out for vengeance. The letters between him and the Empress were now publicly printed as proof that theirs had been an adulterous relationship, and it was even rumoured that he had seduced the young princesses and Anna Vyrubova. The latter made him smile ironically.

"One would have to be hard-pressed to share a bed with such a stupid, docile cow as Anna," he remarked.

Still, he could imagine Nicholas's rage at hearing his beloved wife's name besmirched. No, now would not be a diplomatic time to return to the capital. He must bide his time and wait patiently for the cry of despair that he knew ultimately must come.

It came in October 1912. In August the Royal Family went to their hunting lodge in Bialowieza in Poland, and, despite Derevenko's attentions, the seven-year-old Tsarevitch Alexis fell into a rowing boat and bruised his thigh. For several days Dr Botkin hovered anxiously near by, watching for a haemophiliac reaction as the boy lay in bed, but eventually the bruise subsided and all appeared well. The family moved on to Spala, an ancient Polish hunting seat of the kings.

Alexis was still pale but uncomplaining. One day his mother decided to take him out for a drive in her coach.

"You are so pale, sweetheart. The fresh air will bring colour to your cheeks," she assured him, and, with the boy carefully positioned between herself and Anna so that he should not be jolted, they set off. After a short distance Alexis began to whimper.

"What is it, darling?" the Empress cried in alarm.

"My leg hurts, Mama, and my stomach too."

Alexandra turned pale. "Coachman, turn back to the villa at once! The Tsarevitch is ill!"

The driver obediently turned and retraced their path, but the boy grew paler and began to scream. Alexandra was terrified. Every bump in the road made her child scream with agony.

She hung anxiously over the bed while Botkin examined him.

"How is he? What ails the boy?" she whispered.

Botkin straightened and led her from the bed. "There is a severe haemorrhage, I fear, in the thigh and groin. He needs specialist help."

Alexandra blenched, and fled to her husband. Overnight they summoned Russia's most eminent doctors to Spala—the

128

surgeon Rauchfuss, the pediatrician Ostrogorsky arrived and examined the boy and then spent endless minutes whispering privately amongst themselves. Alexandra watched helplessly while they failed to staunch the bleeding. She could see the blood under the skin in his leg seeping relentlessly and, finding no outlet, growing into a large swelling which spread up his leg into his groin and across his abdomen. Alexis, in moments of consciousness, screamed and drew his leg up against his chest, but the blood flowed on and on.

"Can you not alleviate his pain?" the anguished mother cried, clinging to Botkin's sleeve. "He cannot bear the pain any longer!"

But the doctors shook their heads gravely and did not answer. The boy grew delirious with the pain that wracked his little body, and she stuffed her fingers in her ears to shut out his feeble cry of "O Lord, have mercy on me!"

But wherever she knelt and prayed throughout the building, the child's screams ripped through the walls. For hours on end she sat by his bedside, neither eating nor sleeping, and watched his face grow whiter as the blood left it to engorge his pain yet further.

It was so terrible, so frustrating to be able only to hold his hand and smooth his sweat-soaked golden hair from his eyes as he cried out. Tears flowed down her cheeks as he pleaded with her.

"Mama, help me! Won't you help me?"

"May God help you, baby, for I can't!" she wept.

Tsar Nicholas saw his wife spent and exhausted with watching and weeping, and he took turns to sit with his son. But she could not sleep, even when he relieved her. And often Nicholas, unable to bear the sight of his son in agony, fled from the room weeping and left Alexandra to begin the vigil again.

"He is going to die this time, isn't he, Nicky?" the Empress said on the fifth day. "I know it. He will die unless a miracle happens."

"You must not believe it, darling," the Tsar tried to re-assure her.

Alexandra sat by the boy and watched him awaken from a brief respite of sleep. His blue eyes turned to look at her soberly.

"I am going to die, Mama."

"No, darling! You will recover soon!" Alexandra's terrified voice belied her words.

"No, I shall die. And when I am dead, it will not hurt any more, will it, Mama?"

The Empress sobbed silently. Alexis took her hand in his little shrunken one. "And when I am dead, build me a little monument of stones in the woods."

Alexandra told her husband of their son's words, engulfed in misery and despair. "So soon we are to lose our precious flower, Nicky. It is so cruel. The fate of the Romanovs will not be averted. We are doomed."

Nicholas stiffened. "You must not say such things, beloved. It may come to the ears of the people, and you know how hard we have struggled to keep the boy's illness from them."

"What does it matter now, if he dies?" Alexandra cried. "Nothing matters any more!"

"We can only let it be known that he is ill—no specified illness—and ask for the country's prayers for him," the Tsar pronounced.

And so it was. The official announcement that the Tsarevitch was gravely ill was followed by national prayer in the Cathedral of Our Lady of Kazan and all the churches in the land. Rumours buzzed busily back and forth as to the nature of the illness, and in a London newspaper it was even reported that the Tsarevitch had been badly wounded by a bomb. But Nicholas remained silent, and speculation flourished.

Still the anguished parents hovered over the bed where their dying son lay and wondered what sin they had committed that their child should be forced to suffer such agony. The legend of the curse of the Romanovs seemed inevitable. The boy's pain was now so excruciating as the haematoma engulfed his body that he was barely conscious most of the time. He was beginning to slip out of their reach.

"Send for the priest," Alexandra whispered at last. The royal suite was dismissed and the priest called. The last sacrament of Extreme Unction was administered to the white little figure in the bed, and Nicholas watched his wife's bent figure, the golden hair streaked with grey over the last few days, and wondered how best to word the royal proclamation that His Royal Highness the Tsarevitch was dead.

Alexandra raised her head and turned her red-eyed gaze upon him.

"Only a miracle . . ." she croaked hoarsely.

"My darling, there comes a time when it is past hoping for miracles." He put his arm about her shoulders and felt her shudder.

"Not yet! Not yet, Nicky! There is still time!"

Nicholas glanced at the inert little figure. "Still time? No, my precious, I fear not. We must resign ourselves to God's will, hard though it may be." His voice was choking now.

"No—there is time!" Alexandra's voice was near hysterical. "I shall send for Gregory! He has never failed us yet!"

"Gregory?" The Tsar was bewildered. "But he is hundreds of miles away, in Siberia. He could not arrive in time. Besides, dearest, although he is a holy man, he cannot work such a miracle."

"Do you not remember his words, Nicky, when Alexis was so ill before? 'He will live as long as I am here,' he said. Oh, why did we let him go away? Please—please—let us send for him now before it is too late!"

Nicholas hesitated. "Very well, if you wish it." He did not truly believe a miracle could happen, but if sending for Rasputin would please Alexandra, then he would agree to it. It was difficult for him even to snatch at a straw, so convinced he was of failure and doom for his family. Was he not born on the day of Job, the great sufferer? And had not the prophet Seraphim of Saratov foretold over a century ago that misery, war and rebellion would dog the Tsar who reigned at the beginning of the twentieth century? How could one avoid destiny? Tonight, he felt certain, his son would draw his last breath.

The Empress dispatched Anna Vyrubova with all speed to telegraph Rasputin at Pokrovskoe. "Beg him to pray for my son's life, Anna. Tell him all else has failed."

All night she kept vigil and prayed. In the morning Alexis was still just alive, but unconscious. The doctors stood shaking their heads still, obviously waiting for the last gasp. Alexandra herself felt deathly tired but strangely composed.

Then the telegram arrived. Alexandra read it and felt faint with happiness and relief. Her son was going to live, whatever the doctors said. She went downstairs to the drawing-room. Nicky and the girls were there, their faces white with apprehension as she came in.

"Do not worry, all is well," she said quietly. "I am not a bit anxious any more. Father Gregory has reassured me completely."

Nicholas strode forward and took the piece of paper from

her hand as she sank wearily into a chair, a smile of radiant happiness on her face. He read it aloud to his daughters.

"God has seen your tears and heard your prayers. Do not grieve. The Little One will not die. Do not allow the doctors to bother him too much. Rasputin."

EIGHTEEN

To ALEXANDRA it was no less than a divine miracle, wrought by her saintly friend's direct intervention with God. By mid-morning Alexis opened his eyes and, for the first time in days, he knew her.

"God be praised!" the Empress wept on her knees by his side. They were the clear, bright eyes of the child she loved, no longer clouded by pain and misery. Incredibly the doctors pronounced that all trace of his high fever was gone and the terrible swellings reduced. With careful nursing he would live.

She sat constantly by him as he recovered sufficient strength to sit up, surrounded by pillows. She read to him, and marvelled to see the smile that weakly lit his young face.

"It will take time, a long time, but he will recover," Nicholas said softly. "Heaven be praised."

"And may God bless Rasputin," his wife added.

"Indeed. The holy man is indeed a saint."

Alexandra smiled. Now Nicky was as convinced as herself of Father Gregory's miracle-working powers. Never again need she fear losing him, for Nicholas would never let him go again once he came back to them.

The bruises continued to fade, internally absorbed, and with difficulty Alexis began to move again. In a few weeks he was well enough to be moved back to Tsarskoe Selo. Alexandra was anxious to return to the capital, for by now perhaps Rasputin would have returned there. She had the road to the station specially smoothed and the train ordered to crawl so that there was little chance her precious son would be jolted.

She looked back at the last moment as they were leaving Spala.

"I shall never forget this place, Nicky."

"Nor I, beloved."

She could not put it into words, but she meant that the emotions experienced there had been more than just a mother's anguish. It had been the most profoundly spiritual experience of her life, a deeply moving religious experience in which her faith in God had been supremely strengthened by the works of Father Gregory. What a saint he was! It was only through the power of his prayers that her son was alive, and never, never would she forget it. Anxious times could well come again, but with Gregory by her side she could bear her punishment, the suffering she was bound to endure as a penance for her sin, but without him she was lost. She loved this Siberian peasant and needed him, and now Nicky would see to it that he stayed with them.

Meanwhile the object of her reverent thoughts was making his way back to the capital, his heart bursting with pride and triumph.

"You see, it is as I told you," he said to Praskovie as he kissed her goodbye. "I knew the Empress would send for me."

And now here he was, back in St Petersburg. He would not go back to the house in the Nevsky Prospect, a present from the Grand Duchess who now despised him. He chose instead an apartment in Gorokhovaya Street, five rooms with a front and a more private rear entrance. In the bedroom, simply furnished with a bed, a table, a wash-hand basin and a desk, he arranged about him his treasured possessions. Photographs of the Royal Family, personally signed, he hung on the walls and on the desk he laid the gold watch presented to him by the Tsar, with its engraved cover depicting the arms of the Romanovs.

Word came from Tsarskoe Selo almost at once. The Tsar would be honoured to have him attend. Rasputin drove to the palace proudly. Now all those in the capital who had attacked him so vigorously in his absence could see how necessary he was to the Tsar, for the Royal Family had returned only yesterday.

The Tsarina welcomed him with tearful joy. "My dear, dear friend! God bless you, and I pray we may never be parted again," she sobbed, kissing his hairy hand in gratitude. "My baby lives, thanks to you, and continues to recover. In a year, the doctors say, he may walk again."

Nicholas was no less demonstrative in his thanks, and Rasputin's heart swelled. But he must take care, now that he was reinstated. He voiced his concern bluntly.

"But Nicholas has forbidden the Duma and the press ever to criticise you again!" the Empress cried.

"Nevertheless, I am hated because you love me. Even my own people, the peasants, do not care for the idea of one of their own being so familiar with the Tsar. And I have many stronger enemies here in St Petersburg."

"Then what do you suggest, dear friend?"

"I think it would be wiser that I am not seen here at the palace so often. The hatred against me will only grow and so weaken your cause. It would be best if we do not meet so often."

"No!" Alexandra cried fearfully. "Alexis needs you!"

"I shall be here whenever he needs me, but for the rest of the time I must stay away."

"Oh, Gregory! I need you too! I cannot bear not to see you! Do not be so hard!"

Rasputin fingered his beard thoughtfully. "Then you and I and Batiushka can meet at Anna Vyrubova's house. Even then I shall no doubt be under the surveillance of the Ochrana and those who loathe me, especially those in the Duma."

And so it was agreed, despite the Empress's protests. Even she had to admit that such discretion was wise, for Nicholas's power as the Tsar was still undeniably shaky, as her mother-in-law the Dowager Empress Marie spared no pains to point out.

"Get rid of the fellow!" she urged her daughter-in-law. "You risk Nicky's life, making him appear the creature of such a man."

"I cannot. We need him," Alexandra tried to explain.

"You need your husband more. Do you not realise the danger there is? If Rasputin stays, there are those who would take the opportunity to depose the Tsar. It has happened before."

Alexandra knew it. Three major revolutions had occurred at the palace in the last two hundred years, and two Tsars had lost their lives. But she remained deaf to Marie's pleas.

"Once before I let Rasputin go away, and Alexis nearly died. I shall not send him away again," she said firmly, and Marie left, defeated.

Rasputin did as he suggested, visiting the royal couple infrequently at Anna's, and spending the rest of his time drinking and debauching as before and receiving guests at his house. Suppliants came again by the score, and such was the easy manner of his style of living that anyone who wished could stay to sit at his dining table for supper. Rasputin's housekeeper, a distant cousin named Dunya, showed never a sign of impatience on her plump, homely face as she cooked for innumerable visitors, and a constant smell of cooking and wet washing hung about the house.

Many visitors were outright beggars seeking money or a new overcoat. Many were sick folk seeking the miraculous cure they heard Rasputin had often performed, and many more were women anxious to see for themselves the hypnotic charmer over whom other women had gone into raptures. He disappointed none of them. Food, cases of madeira, caviare, money and many parcels, even carpets, appeared on the steps of his back door in token of gratitude, for he would charge no fee for his services.

And many of his visitors, arriving in closed carriages and climbing the stairs cautiously, came to enlist his support for their advancement. Cheerfully he wrote out slips of paper to help them secure official positions, minor ones usually, as most ministerial-level officers were his enemies. His notes, scrawled with some difficulty, consisted only of a few words such as "Do it for me, there's a good fellow! Rasputin." And the bearer of the note would usually return to say the request had been carried out.

His popularity appeared to be waxing again, judging by the constant flow of people to his door. But he was not deceived. He knew as clearly as if he had seen it that his enemies watched every move, even his visits to mass and his now rarer visits to the palace to talk and joke with the children and embrace his dear friends Alexandra and Nicholas were carefully reported. He knew the names of some of the men he must beware of—Kokovtsov, the Prime Minister, and Rodzianko, the new president of the Duma, for certain. Both men resented his power over the royal pair.

And early in the New Year, 1913, Rasputin came briefly into open conflict with Rodzianko. The Tsar and Tsarina were preparing for a series of magnificent celebrations in honour of the tercentenary of the Romanov dynasty, and he knew how earnestly the Tsar hoped he could reinstate himself in the love of his people by public appearances. The celebrations were to begin with a Te Deum in the Kazan Cathedral, with the

Royal Family, foreign ambassadors and government ministers and members of the Duma present.

Rasputin heard how Rodzianko had been displeased with the rear seats offered to the Duma, and argued until better seats at the front were procured for them. The holy man smiled maliciously to himself as he dressed himself in his best crimson tunic, his black cloth trousers and patent leather boots and the heavy gold cross and chain the Empress had given him. Then before the royal couple arrived he slipped past the guard protecting the Duma seats, and sat down. From the corner of his eye he watched the sergeant hesitate, then go to whisper to Rodzianko.

"A peasant? Where?" Rodzianko demanded.

The sergeant pointed to Rasputin and Rodzianko reddened. He crossed to Rasputin, his huge face burning with anger, and towered over the seated figure.

"You—out!" he said, in as near a roar as the hushed atmosphere of the cathedral would permit.

Rasputin looked up at him mildly.

"You heard me! Get out! These are seats reserved for members of the Duma."

Rasputin waited, but the man was not so enraged as to be foolish enough to add that though Rasputin's power in the land was great, he was no Duma member. He was too shrewd. Rasputin withdrew a card from his pocket.

"I have an invitation to attend from the Tsar himself," he said politely.

"You may sit elsewhere, but not here. Do you hear me— go!"

Rasputin shook his head firmly and stared into the man's eyes. Deliberately he made his pupils contract, and fixed Rodzianko with the look that had conquered many, but

Rodzianko shifted uneasily for a moment and then averted his gaze.

"Go—or I'll drag you from the cathedral by your beard," the big man spat, his eyes glistening with fury.

"Oh! Such violence!" Rasputin protested, and falling to his knees he began to pray. Rodzianko's face became purple.

"Out! Out! Out!" he roared, and heads all around the vast church turned anxiously. The Tsar and Tsarina would be arriving at any moment. "Get out!" And as Rodzianko's temper gave way, he began kicking Rasputin viciously in the ribs. "Enough of this tomfoolery! Go away!" He grasped Rasputin by the scruff of his neck.

Rasputin looked up from his prayers reproachfully and began to rise. Rodzianko let go of him and stood back to let him pass. Disapproving voices murmured all about them in outrage.

Rasputin paused in the aisle, certain that every eye in the cathedral was upon him. "Lord, forgive him his sin," he murmured, loud enough for it to carry to all the four corners.

Afterwards Rasputin laughed over the incident. "He came off worst, I think," he confided to the Empress in Anna's drawing-room.

"I don't know," the Tsar said doubtfully. "Rodzianko feels he scored a major victory over you."

"We shall see," Rasputin laughed softly.

"But was it wise to make an enemy of a man so powerful, dear friend?" Alexandra said doubtfully.

"He is known as a braggart, and few will believe his version. Those who saw it will draw a different conclusion," Rasputin replied confidently. "But let us talk of other matters. What is the next event in the celebrations?"

"Oh—a grand reception at the Winter Palace tomorrow," Alexandra replied wearily.

140

"And the opera at the Maryinsky Theatre," added Nicholas.

"And then the journey to the Upper Volga in May." Alexandra's voice sounded even more tired, but she seemed to notice it and added more brightly, "Then your people will really see you, Nicholas, and you will see how they love you. It is all nonsense about the unrest in the country, you will see. Is that not so, Gregory?"

"I agree it is a good idea to strengthen a relationship which may have grown weaker through absence," Rasputin said guardedly.

"And you will be there on the journey with us to see it, dear friend, will you not?" the Tsarina finished triumphantly.

NINETEEN

NICHOLAS and Alexandra had good reason to be delighted with their pilgrimage to the Upper Volga, to visit the birthplace of the Romanov dynasty where Michael Romanov was born three centuries earlier. The sixteen-year-old boy had been elected in 1613 by the Russian national assembly, the Zemsky Sobor, from among the many claimants and pretenders to fill the throne left vacant by Ivan the Terrible.

Now the royal couple were retracing his route to the throne. Alexandra was overjoyed at the tumultuous reception they received all along the route. Peasants lined the banks, even wading waist-high in the water to acclaim the boat in which their Tsar sat. People stopped work to rush down to the river and cheer themselves hoarse.

"You see, dear friend, we are loved by our people," Alexandra remarked contentedly to Rasputin on their return. "They love us because they know we love them."

"So it would seem, Matushka," Rasputin replied.

"All those stories our ministers told us about the peasants being half-starved and blaming us were untrue. They didn't look at all hungry, and as for blaming us—why, you should have heard how they cheered us! Probably it was only that they did not know us. We had only to show ourselves and at once their hearts were ours."

Rasputin refrained from commenting that as a peasant himself he knew a peasant's pride. They would not demonstrate their hunger on a river bank. Cheering and shouting only served to veil for a moment the gnawing pain inside. And

142

generations of religious belief made Russian peasants revere their Tsar as their God, but latterly that faith was beginning to crack. Less than a year ago a drunken police officer had ordered his men to fire on a peaceful column of strikers in the Lena goldfields, with the result that two hundred innocent people had died, and yet the Duma had hushed the matter and exonerated the police. And still matters were growing worse. Seven hundred thousand workers in Russia were on strike and the likelihood was that the number would grow far higher yet. Hungry bellies would not stay silent for ever.

Then there was the rapidly-growing feeling of antagonism towards Austria and her land-grabbing policy in the Balkans which was developing now into hysterical war-fever. Feelings were running high against Austria, especially in the capital, and Rasputin could feel the rumblings which threatened to rock the nation. Despite Alexandra's optimism, he feared for the country's safety, and more especially for the Tsar's.

Looking about him in St Petersburg, he could see no sign of apprehension. The society about him was effete and decadent, caught up in a maelstrom of feverish activity as if completely unaware of the eddying unrest outside. The shop windows blazed with lights as jostling customers thronged the streets, elegant ladies opined in their luxury hairdressing salons what Madame This or That might be wearing at the ball at the Anitchkov Palace tonight. Nijinski was dancing in "Giselle", and the most excited gossip was about his scandalous costume which resulted in his being expelled from the Imperial Ballet. No one seemed to give a thought to impending war or rebellion and their repercussions.

Rasputin shook his head. It was his people, the peasants, who suffered the terrible burden and sacrifices of war, not the wealthy and the boyars. He had done his best, warning the

Tsar against war as he had done once before in 1908, but his voice was one of very few.

"Think what will become of you and your people," he said to Nicholas. "Your grandfather helped Bulgaria to shake off the Turkish yoke, and how did they repay their saviour, Little Mother Russia? Will our fathers, who shed their blood for these treacherous Tartars, bless their sons if you send them on this campaign? They say we must help our Slav brothers, but was not Cain the brother of Abel?"

His appeal at least impressed the Tsar sufficiently to delay the onset of war. But for how long? Instead of brooding, Rasputin returned to his former mode of life in the city. Nightly excursions to the dram-shops to consume vast quantities of wine and then on to the brothels or the Villa Rode Cabaret alternated with daily tea-parties. Droshkas and the newfangled invention, cars, would line the street outside his house in the Gorokhovaya each afternoon while their lady occupants climbed the stairs to his flat to drink tea and commune with him.

One afternoon he sat at table presiding over the samovar and surrounded by a circle of admiring society ladies. There was a tap at the door and the housekeeper Dunya admitted a young woman in a kerchief. Rasputin heard the indrawn gasps of his guests, but ignored them.

"Come in, Tanya. You are welcome here. Please sit and join us." It gave him pleasure to see the elegantly-behatted ladies have to make room for the common woman. She sat down timidly and hung her head, making no effort to speak.

"You were saying, Father, about the benefits which may come from sin," an anxious lady prompted him. Rasputin turned his gaze on her.

"I was saying, my child, that one may sin as a child, or as a youth, or even as an adult, and then repent. The time comes to turn to God. But how can one repent as a child before one knows what sin is? One must experience it, and then repent. Turning to God and surrendering one's thoughts to Him utterly, one becomes His creature. Then you may sin again, for it is a special kind of sin. And one may be freed of it over and over again. Thus everything is good. Do you understand?"

It was obvious from their blank faces that they had followed not a word, but since it was such devious and illogical reasoning, how could they? He glanced at Tanya. She was gazing about her at her surroundings. He followed her gaze. She was looking at the ikon by the window, the picture of the Cathedral of St Isaac, hung with bright ribbons. Then her attention turned to the table laden with tarts and fruit, black bread and gherkins, jam and boiled eggs and a bottle of wine.

"A glass of tea, Tanya?" he said in an effort to capture her attention. His theological talk had evidently gone right over her head. Tanya shook her head and looked down humbly. Obviously she was overwhelmed by the presence of so many society ladies. He wondered curiously what had brought her here.

He pushed plates of cakes and cracknels towards the ladies and watched with an amused smile as they tackled them delicately with a fork. Unhesitatingly he broke open a boiled egg messily with his bare hands and smiled to see how they averted their gaze politely as he wiped the yellow yolk from his fingers on to the tablecloth.

"And you, little one," he said, turning to stroke the cheek of a pretty, fair-haired newcomer to the circle. "Have you come to be initiated?"

She blushed and smiled. It did not escape his notice that several of the other women's eyes lit up in expectation. They had been initiated and knew the delights.

"Yes," he murmured thoughtfully to the fair one. "I believe

145

you are ready for conversion, for I detect a distinct aura of piety about you. Are you ready to commune with your Lord?"

There was rapid breathing discernible in his audience. The girl shrieked gently and ran from the room. Rasputin smiled. Then he saw Tanya's face watching him wide-eyed. She was still a very attractive woman, though she must be in her thirties now, he estimated. Why had she come today?

"Enough for today," he said abruptly, rising to signify to his listeners that he had done with them. Groans of disappointment filled the air, and the clatter of rosary beads being stowed away into handbags.

"Are you offended with us, Father?" a plump, elderly lady heavily bedecked with jewels asked him. "Do we not learn and understand your teachings quickly enough? We love you and long only to hear and please you."

"No. I have other matters to attend to. Good day to you all."

"Please give us your blessing then, before we go."

Rasputin raised his hand to make the sign of the cross. Instantly several of the women fell to their knees devoutly, some touching the hem of his caftan. Then they stood again and waited expectantly. Rasputin kissed two of them full on the lips while some of the women kissed each other fervently, gathered up their coats and wraps and hovered by the door, reluctant to leave.

Rasputin saw the young woman who snatched up some rusks from the table as a souvenir, and heard the over-loud voices outside talking to Dunya as they left, begging her for some of his soiled linen to wash.

"Such an honour, for the Master. Please let me take it today!"

"Let me have one piece only, then—the dirtiest, the sweatiest you can find, Dunya!"

146

Tanya made to follow the ladies out. Rasputin signalled her to stay. She sat in a corner chair again and waited until the chattering voices had died away. Rasputin crossed slowly to her, looked down and took her face in his hands.

"Why have you come, Tanya?"

"I have heard so many stories about you. I wanted to see for myself."

"Is that all? Are you satisfied?"

She smiled. "What I have seen only confirms what I already knew—that you are a holy man and all the rest is lies. But I came also because I wanted to warn you."

"Warn me? Of what?"

"My husband—Serge, you remember? He is a Cossack. We married two years ago and we are happy with our son. But Serge is in the Imperial Guard, and he hears things. He has heard rumours that powerful men are determined to destroy you. Oh, I am so afraid for you, Gregory!"

He stroked her cheek gently. "There is no need to fear for me, child. Do not fret yourself."

"But you are so good—you do not recognise the evil in other men's hearts! You walk in ignorance of your danger, Gregory!"

Rasputin sighed and turned away. "Unfortunately, I know only too well that I am hated and reviled, Tanya, and that there are those who plan my downfall. But I continue in the light of God's words to me, doing the work I am destined to do."

Tanya sighed in admiration. "How good and kind you are! Your people are so proud of you. It is gratifying to us to see a peasant like ourselves risen to the ranks of the highest in the land, just as it has always been foretold. Russia's salvation, they say, will be achieved by a man of the people. But how can you let them lie about you the way they do?"

147

Rasputin shrugged. "Let them say what they will. What does it matter if I am rumoured to mesmerise the Tsarevitch, to bribe that stupid bitch Anna to poison him so that I only appear to cure him, that I am evil and debauched and dance naked in the streets? What does it matter? The Son of God is always reviled and misrepresented."

"Oh, Gregory!" Tanya was entranced by his pious words. Then she wriggled nervously. "Only Serge does not know you as I do, and he thinks they will do something terrible to you, and justifiably so, he thinks. What am I to do, Gregory?"

He took her hands. "Go home, and do not fret. What is to be, will be."

"But if I hear through Serge of any plan . . ."

"You will do as God directs you, child. Now go. So many troubles vex my spirit. I am in need of physical exertion to dispel them. I shall go to the Villa Rode and dance and dance as we did round the log fires in Siberia, until I am exhausted. Perhaps then my mind will be more at peace. Go now."

He kissed her gently on the forehead and watched her make a quick, apologetic sign of the cross before she slipped quickly out.

But as the old year faded and the new year of 1914 loomed over Russia, Rasputin still felt uneasy. War clouds still hovered threateningly, and more and more of Russia's millions were out of work. Conditions were shaping themselves quickly and inevitably for a critical situation, and Rasputin sensed the débacle that was to come.

Then when the Tsar suddenly dismissed his Prime Minister Kokovtsov and replaced him with the aged, feeble Goremykin, Russia's instability was even greater. The Tsar, backed by Rasputin, argued with the Duma and seriously thought of disbanding it. Rasputin's enemies multiplied. And when the Grand Duke Nichcolas openly joined the anti-Rasputin faction by stolidly refusing to attend the Tsar's Easter banquet and sit at the same table as the peasant charlatan, the Tsar's temper snapped. He angrily ordered his uncle to attend.

"Do not compel him, Batiushka," Rasputin said when the Tsar told him of the incident. "I know he plans my ruin, but in doing so he will come to grief himself."

The Grand Duke did not appear at the royal table on Easter Sunday. The news spread rapidly about the capital and all St Petersburg society split itself instantly into pro- and anti-Rasputin factions. The newspapers, ignoring the Tsar's ban, openly championed the Grand Duke's challenge.

Rasputin began to feel that he was sitting on a powder-keg. His safety, he felt, would be better served by his temporary absence from the city. Accordingly he told Nicholas and Alexandra.

Alexandra wept. "Do not desert us now, dear friend! We have need of you."

Rasputin cleared his throat. "Unfortunately, there are those here in powerful positions who are jealous of your love for me. They are too stupid to know that the Voice of God speaks to you through me, and that I am here to protect you and your royal house. They would destroy that love and deceive their Tsar. I do not wish to be the cause of harm to you both, and therefore I must leave you, for a time at least."

Nicholas coughed. "Must you go, starets? For the love of Christ, stay and help us."

Rasputin shook his head sadly. "I am tired from my work and need rest. But I shall return when you need me."

Alexandra burst into floods of tears and covered his hands with kisses, imploring him to change his mind. But Rasputin was resolute. In May he set off on the journey home to Pokrovskoe.

TWENTY

THE presentiments that weighed on Rasputin's heart were not long in being fulfilled. Within weeks of his leaving St Petersburg the Damocletian sword that had remained so long quiveringly suspended, fell. Its victims in quick succession were the Tsarevitch Alexis, Rasputin himself, and the middle-aged Archduke Franz Ferdinand, heir to the Austrian throne.

The starets, happily reunited with his family in Pokrovskoe, went out one afternoon to send a telegram to the Empress, who was holidaying with her family in Livadia. As he walked along the dusty, sunlit village street in his flowing caftan, he was totally unaware of the fate that threatened him.

A young woman suddenly appeared before him and looked at him accusingly. "Gregory Efimovitch Rasputin?" she challenged.

Rasputin nodded graciously. Another suppliant. They were never far away. He reached into the pocket of his caftan for a coin. Before he could withdraw his hand, he saw her arm suddenly rise in the air, the June sunlight glistening on a long blade, then the swift arc of its descent, and he felt a sickening feeling as the cold steel raked into his entrails. Stunned and bewildered, he felt her whip the knife clear, raise it and stab him again.

"Who—are—you?" he gasped, excruciating pain searing through his guts. "And—why?"

"I am Khina Guseva, sent by Iliodor to rid the world of Anti-Christ!" she shrieked, her venomous eyes glittering with triumph. "I have done it! I have slain Anti-Christ!"

150

People came running then and seized the young woman. Rasputin clutched at his abdomen, pressing his fists into the gaping wound to stem the flow of blood and, rejecting offers of help, he staggered homewards in a mist of pain.

Praskovie, horrified, sent for the doctor. It took eight hours for him to drive from Tiumen by carriage and by then Rasputin was collapsed and near to death. The surgeon had no time to lose.

"Scrub the table," he ordered Praskovie curtly, and there, by candlelight, he operated on the holy man's wounds. Praskovie hovered close by, tense and terrified. At length the surgeon wiped the sweat from his brow. "Now we must wait and pray," he said, and washed his bloodstained hands.

Rasputin, with his sturdy peasant body and massive will to live, survived. In a day or two he was sufficiently strong to be moved to the hospital at Tiumen.

"But make no mistake," the doctor warned Praskovie, "it will be many weeks yet before he is strong again. Those wounds uncovered his entrails completely."

Rasputin recovered slowly. In hospital he heard how the peasants had wanted to lynch Khina Guseva, but he intervened on her behalf. Instead of being brought to trial, she was found to be insane and committed to a lunatic asylum. Rasputin lay in his hospital bed and thanked God he was alive. This time at least he had cheated his enemies of their plan to destroy him.

Nicholas and Alexandra, holidaying far away on the Baltic coast, were completely unaware of their dear friend's terrible mishap. Alexandra was smiling on the quayside as they waited to board the imperial yacht, the *Standart*.

"Take care now, Alexis," she warned her son. The nine-year-old boy seemed at last to be fully recovered from his illness at Spala eighteen months ago, but one still had to exercise great care. Alexis smiled impishly and leapt for the boarding ladder. His foot caught awkardly on one of the rungs and he gasped as he twisted his ankle.

"Are you hurt, darling?" his mother cried anxiously.

"No, Mama. It is nothing."

Reassured by his calmness and no evidence of injury, Alexandra ordered the voyage to continue. Once or twice during the evening she saw Alexis grimacing, but in answer to her concerned enquiries, he insisted that all was well.

By morning it was evident that Alexis was indeed hurt. The bruise on his ankle was haemorrhaging and the joint was swollen and rigid. Alexis was weeping continuously, and by afternoon he was screaming with pain.

Alexandra went white-faced to her husband's cabin.

"Nicky, my dearest. Alexis is ill. We must act quickly. For God's sake send for Father Gregory! We must not leave it until Alexis is dying again. Telegraph Gregory in Pokrovskoe at once!" She looked at her husband, sitting white and motionless at his desk. "Nicky! Do you hear me?"

"Yes, sweetheart. But I have just received other news which takes my breath away."

"News? What news could be so important as this?"

"The Archduke Franz Ferdinand of Austria was assassinated in Sarajevo yesterday."

"Franz Ferdinand? The heir to the throne of Austria? Well, what is that to us? They are our enemies, are they not, and of what account are their troubles when our own son is so ill?" Alexandra waved her long, thin hands in agitation. Why waste time on politics when there was such a crisis to face?

Nicholas sighed patiently, and his look was far-away.

"Yes, they are our enemies. But the Archduke and his wife Sophie were shot by a Serb, a boy named Gabriel Princip. In the Bosnian capital too, and of course the Austrians are crying out for vengeance. It could mean war, Alex darling, and the world will look to Russia for a lead."

"Oh, no, it will not lead to war, Nicky, I know it will not. But please, forget it for a moment and send for Rasputin quickly before it is too late."

Nicholas took one look at his wife's stricken face and agreed. Almost at once word was brought back to the *Standart* that Rasputin had been knifed and was lying in hospital fighting for his life. Alexandra was beside herself with grief, but as the yacht turned about and the Royal Family made their way back to the capital, her anxiety over her son diminished. His ankle was still swollen and painful, but the fever had gone and he was recovering.

Alexandra breathed a sigh of relief and left her husband in peace to conduct his affairs. Back in St Petersburg he was immediately taken up by the state visit of the French President Poincaré. At the end of the four days of balls and concerts and banquets Poincaré sailed for home. Austria then delivered an ultimatum to the Serbs.

It was carefully timed so that Nicholas and Poincaré were no longer together to plan Russian and French reaction. Serbia turned to Russia at once, as her traditional champion, and Nicholas replied that he still hoped to avert war. He summoned all his ministers to Tsarskoe Selo to deliberate.

"My sincere desire is for peace," he told the assembled sombre-eyed men, "but at the same time we cannot be indifferent to Serbia's fate."

"But it is a threat aimed directly at us if we fail to intervene," the Foreign Minister Sazonov pointed out. The Grand Duke Nicholas, Inspector General of the Army, murmured his agreement.

"Your Majesty personally has guaranteed Serbian independence, and any threat to that can be interpreted only as a challenge to our influence in the Balkans. We must act."

"Frankly, I regret it," Sazonov continued, "because it will no doubt mean that other countries will be involved. *C'est la guerre européenne*. But it cannot be avoided. We lose our position as a great power if we permit Serbia to be humiliated thus."

Other heads nodded gravely in agreement. Nicholas felt bewildered. So long he had prayed to avoid war which could mean not only a threat to his throne, but to Russia herself. But there was no one there to speak against war. The one man who would have argued fiercely and perhaps have delayed or even avoided the momentous decision was lying near to death in Tiumen hospital.

So when, three days later, Austria issued a declaration of war against Serbia, he had no choice but to order all Russian military districts along the Austrian frontier to mobilise.

His cousin Wilhelm, Kaiser of Germany, was furious and refused to mediate. Sazonov urged a reluctant Tsar to order a general mobilisation at once. Nicholas turned pale.

"Think of the responsibility. . . . It would mean sending hundreds of thousands of Russian people to their deaths."

His face betrayed the terrible inner struggle he was enduring. If only Rasputin were here to help and advise him. At last he spoke.

"Very well. There is nothing left for us to do but get ready for an attack. Give my order for general mobilisation."

Germany at once declared war on Russia. At once Nicholas felt calm and resolved. If his own cousin had failed him, then at least the path was clear. He had a responsibility to his people and a duty to God to perform, and, however onerous, he set out unflinchingly to perform it.

Following the ancient tradition that all Russian tsars began a war by going to Moscow, to the Kremlin, to seek God's blessing, Nicholas and his family journeyed to Moscow in August. Crowds cheered hoarsely, lining the streets and hanging from trees and balconies to watch. The country seethed in a state of patriotic fervour, anxious to demonstrate their love and loyalty. Nicholas and Alexandra were overjoyed at the spontaneous and overwhelming display. The people believed in Russia's supremacy and were eager to protect it. Nicholas felt a quiet pride and justification.

Rasputin was still unconscious in hospital when the momentous decision was taken. By the time he could sit up and understand, Russian troops were marching into Prussia. The blood of many nationalities was seeping inexorably into the soil. Thousands of Russian peasants, under their Commander-in-Chief, Grand Duke Nicholas, were already defeated and butchered. Rasputin blazed with anger at the loss of so many of his countrymen.

"The fool!" he muttered furiously in his bed. "I warned him once before the Balkans were not worth fighting for!" And despite his weakness he demanded pen and paper and sat up in bed to write a laborious, fateful warning to the Tsar.

"Dear Friend,
    I will say again a menacing cloud is over Russia. Lots of sorrow and grief. It is dark and there is no lightening to be seen. A sea of tears immeasurable, and as to blood . . . What can I say? There are no words, the horror of it is indescribable. I know they keep wanting war from you, evidently not knowing that this is destruction. Heavy is God's punishment when he takes away reason, that is the beginning of the end. You are the Tsar, Father of the People. Don't allow the madmen to triumph and destroy themselves and the People. Well, they will

155

conquer Germany, and what about Russia? If one thinks then verily there has not been a greater sufferer since the beginning of time. She is all drowned in blood. Terrible is the destruction and without end the grief.

Gregory."

"It is true," remarked the Empress when Nicholas showed her the letter. "And but for his accident this war would have been averted. You would have listened to him. He was sent by God to advise you. Ah, I am full of foreboding, Nicky. I feel that fate will overwhelm us."

Nicholas did his best to reassure her, but he felt far from confident himself. Then Rasputin returned to St Petersburg, pale and still weak, but with fire enough inside him to rage at the Tsar.

"The generals do not care how many peasants are killed," he roared, "but the vengeance of God will be terrible."

"All my ministers advocated the war," Nicholas protested weakly. He was beginning to vacillate, to doubt the rightness of his action after all.

"Not Count Witte! He was abroad at the time!"

"But Sazonov and Sukhomlinov and Grand Duke Nicholas Nicholaievitch . . ."

"Fools all!" Rasputin roared.

"I tried to tell Nicky you would not approve," the Empress cut in quickly. "If only you had been here! Oh, Gregory! Do not despise us! We need you so much. I feel so alone and friendless now. . . ."

She referred of course to her German birth. She knew many people suspected her now of pro-German sympathies, though in truth she was very proud of the Russian people.

"I am not ashamed of what I have done," Nicholas asserted stoutly. "There are obligations a Tsar cannot ignore."

"Even though he annihilates his own people in the process?" Rasputin demanded, his eyes steely with anger and determination. "The German horde sweeps through our army of peasants like a scythe, hacking them down ruthlessly. Will you let it go on?"

Nicholas coughed deprecatingly and turned away. "I must go to the front myself, to see how Nicholas Nicolaievitch fares." He did not want to talk of the possibility of Russian defeat. He knew only too well how unprepared his country was for war.

Alexandra paled. "To Baranovichi? But it is dangerous, my love!"

"It is essential for morale and to see and talk with Nicholas how things progress. But it will be only a visit, have no fear."

But his visits to the military camp grew longer and more protracted. Alexandra wrote often to him, urging him to listen to Rasputin's advice.

"Rely on the advice of our friend Rasputin. Just a little more confidence in the prayers and help of our friend, and everything will be all right. Let yourself be guided by him, and by God through him."

Alexandra's anxiety over her husband mounted suddenly into terrified panic when on one of his visits home he announced calmly that he was to return to the front, taking the eleven-year-old Tsarevitch with him. The Empress pleaded in vain.

"One day he will sit on the throne in my place," Nicholas told her firmly. "He has led a restricted life until now and needs to have his education widened. But rest in peace, dear heart, I shall take good care of him."

Rasputin grunted and went home to his flat in the Gorokhovaya.

TWENTY-ONE

ANNA VYRUBOVA sat in the train which was taking her back from St Petersburg to Tsarskoe Selo. It had been a happy day, visiting her parents, but she was anxious to return now to her dear friend Alexandra.

She shivered and huddled deeper into her fur cloak, watching the eddying snowflakes swirl and then fade as they slid down the window. The Empress would be watching for her return, anxious to pour out her day's worries and tribulations. Poor Alexandra! She was so sad these days, bereft of her husband and her beloved son. She tried hard to busy herself doing hospital work, but still she fretted and worried. If it were not for dear Father Gregory, always at her side, advising and consoling, the poor Empress might well have had a breakdown by now. He had been so solicitous, helping her with the monumental taks of governing home affairs in the dear Tsar's absence. But for his suggestions they would have been greatly at a loss to know which ministers to appoint in such a time of crisis.

Alexandra leaned heavily on him and he, dear man, had worked and advised without respite, giving her all his time and attention without murmur. What a saintly creature he was, to give of himself so unstintingly and without hope of reward. Not that Father Gregory looked for reward, she corrected herself quickly. He was too noble, too altruistic to care about material gain. He saw in Alexandra a human soul in suffering, and he gave his help as a holy man should. That was all, bless him.

Dear Alexandra! She was so kind and gentle herself that she deserved a friend such as he. She had been so compassionate over Anna's broken marriage, taking her to her heart as a true friend. Anna shuddered as she recalled her husband. What a beast he had been! He had tried so hard to rape her, but in vain.

She looked at the reflection of herself in the carriage window, and saw the plain, heavy face that stared back. Here she was, thirty years old and looking like a maiden aunt already. There was the sting of it. She was a virgin, and likely to remain so until she died.

She smiled sadly and pulled herself together. Still, there was nothing to complain about. No other woman in the whole of Russia could describe herself as the Empress's trusted friend and confidante. She knew everything that touched Alexandra's life, for the Empress told her all. That was an honour indeed.

The train lurched a little. Anna gazed out into the late afternoon darkness to see where they were, but nothing could be seen but the still swirling snow. Suddenly, without any warning, there was an enormous crash, the carriage appeared to rise vertically into the air, the lights went out, and there was a terrible sound of ripping, crashing metal.

Something slashed across Anna's legs, making her scream aloud with the force of the pain. Almost immediately the world turned upside down and a hideous red flash exploded inside her skull, and for Anna all the world disappeared into blackness.

The officials who ran along the snowbound track in the darkness, overwhelmed by the chaos caused by two colliding trains, found her half-crushed body in the debris. She was just alive, but her legs, trapped under heavy steel beams, were shattered. A girder across her face had damaged her skull and her spine, and the carriage, in which she was travelling alone, was completely split in two.

The surgeon at the hospital examined the crushed body briefly.

"Do not disturb her. She is dying," he told the hospital attendants, and turned to the next casualty.

The Empress was informed and Anna Vyrubova was left to die.

Rasputin was at tea with Countess Witte and some other friends when the news came. He borrowed the Countess's car and drove furiously to the hospital. Demanding to be allowed in, he strode to Anna's bedside and looked down at the pulped, unconscious face.

"Annushka! Annushka! Annushka!" he called.

Anna moaned and moved.

"Wake up and rise!" he ordered her loudly, bending his face close to hers. Her eyes opened, and their glances met. Rasputin channelled all the strength in his body into his gaze, and saw Anna's eyes gleam faintly with recognition. She moved again with a tremendous effort.

"Speak to me, Anna."

She moaned indistinguishable sounds, and Rasputin turned to the people standing watching.

"She will recover," he pronounced slowly. "She will live, but she will remain a cripple."

Then he lumbered from the ward, his great body staggering as though drunk. But in truth he was immensely weary, perspiring and dizzy. Every ounce of strength had been drained from his body in the effort to save her. Outside the door, he collapsed.

As Anna slowly recovered and was able to sit in a wheelchair, the Empress marvelled once again at the miraculous powers of her holy friend. Now beyond doubt he was established in her mind as the utterly pure and pious man of God, a peasant sprung from Russian soil to be Russia's salvation. More and more gladly she listened to his every word of advice, and persuaded her husband to do the same. Obstinately she refused to consider reports on his depravity, even an authentic account by the Commander of the Police, Dzhunkovsky. The unfortunate commander was dismissed for his efficiency.

Rasputin lay on the fox bedspread covering his narrow bed and smiled. As with Dzhunkovsky, so perish all who might impeach him. Now he could do with the Empress as he wished. Ministers could topple and be replaced at his whim, for Tsar Nicholas, however he might demur at first, always acceded to his beloved wife's requests in the end.

"There is no end to what I could achieve," he muttered aloud to the glass chandelier. "The Empress is growing weaker physically from all her work, and weak in the head too. I can get her to make the Tsar dissolve the Duma, get rid of that wretch Rodzianko, and then internal affairs are ours to govern. Then dispose of that fool Grand Duke Nicholas, get the Tsar to appoint himself Commander-in-Chief of the Army, and then military strength too is ours to command."

He chuckled aloud at the thought. None of it was wishful thinking, for he knew that through the Tsarina he could achieve it all. He stood to gain nothing from the venture except the grandiose feeling of power, of being able to manipulate all, even the highest, like a set of wooden puppets. He, a Siberian peasant, able to dictate the path of Russia!

But then, he reminded himself soberly, he did as he was bidden by his inner voice, and that voice undoubtedly came from God. Who was he to oppose God's will? No, he must carry out the duties set for him, with all his strength. He was aware he had many enemies now, powerful men who could be a threat to his life at any moment of the day or night. But God would provide for him; He would watch over him as He had always done.

The Grand Duke was the first to fall. He was falling into disfavour over the defeat of Warsaw in August 1915, and his efficiency as Commander-in-Chief of the Army was coming into question. Rasputin offered to come to headquarters to help. Grand Duke Nicholas, bitterly offended by the upstart, replied sharply.

"Yes, do come," his telegraph said, "and I'll hang you."

Showing the note to the Empress was enough. She began endless persuasive letters to Nicholas which culminated in Grand Duke Nicholas being relieved and transferred to the Caucasian front, and the Tsar himself took charge of the army. The nation waited and prayed. After the bloody massacre suffered by the army up to now in the war, perhaps there would be a change for the better.

By degrees Rasputin had his way. Through Alexandra he had the aged, feeble Goremykin dismissed from the post of Prime Minister and his own choice, Sturmer, was appointed. Soon afterwards, Sazonov, the Foreign Minister, was dismissed and his post was also filled by Sturmer. Now all that remained was to get his own man into the most important post of all, the Minister of the Interior.

Rasputin now turned his attention to Russia's military affairs, again working through the easily-malleable Empress. The Cabinet and the Duma were first incredulous and gradually furious at his pretensions, and began to plan how they could rid themselves of the troublemaker and his tool, the Tsarina. Hatred of him and the Empress became more and more openly expressed, particularly as the war was still going badly. The well-to-do citizens of the capital flung themselves even more feverishly into the frenetic social whirl in an effort to forget the war existed, but pessimism, gloom and hatred still filled the St Petersburg air.

Rasputin continued his round of afternoon tea-parties and nightly debauches in between his advisory visits to the Empress. He too felt the gloom and pessimism that filled all hearts.

"Enemies all about me, and they think I cannot see what they plan, but they are transparent to my eyes," he murmured to himself as he sprawled on his bed.

There was Hvostov, for instance. The Minister of the Interior had to go. Rasputin knew full well the harm he plotted, as clearly as he had been able to see as a child when another boy hid a stone behind his back to fling at his unwary victim. Hvostov loathed Rasputin. But the wily starets foresaw the Minister's plan and Hvostov's bungled attempt succeeded only in poisoning Rasputin's cat. His attempt to involve the exiled Iliodor in a conspiracy to murder had also misfired, and Rasputin smiled wryly.

"Give it time. Very soon the rat will be mangled by one of his own vermin," he murmured. And so it was. The Chief of Police, Beletski, turned traitor on Hvostov, revealing his murder plan to the Prime Minister. Hvostov was dismissed in dire disgrace, three days after banishing Beletski to outer Siberia.

Rasputin shrugged his big peasant shoulders. They could all come and go, but he was indestructible. Now he could choose his own Minister of the Interior. He chose Protopopov, a nobody with no particular qualifications for the post, and the little man was delighted. He at least would be a willing slave, and Tsarist autocracy would have nothing to fear from him. Rasputin had difficulty in keeping him in office, however, for the Duma, led by Trepov, fought to be rid of him. It had taken all Alexandra's persuasions to make the Tsar keep him in office.

"I entreat you, don't go and change Protopopov now," she wrote earnestly to her husband. "Change nobody now, otherwise the Duma will think they have succeeded. . . . It's a question of the monarchy and your prestige now . . . Don't think they will stop at him, but will make all others leave who are devoted to you . . . and then ourselves. Remember, the Tsar rules and not the Duma."

When her persuasions prevailed and Protopopov was retained, Alexandra wrote triumphantly again.

"I am fully convinced that great and beautiful times are coming for your reign and Russia . . . We must give a strong country to Baby and dare not be weak for his sake . . . You have to suffer for faults in the reigns of your predecessors, and God knows what hardships are yours. Let our legacy be a lighter one for Alexis . . . Russia loves to feel the whip—it's their nature—tender love and then the iron hand to punish and guide . . . Be Peter the Great, Ivan the Terrible, Emperor Paul—crush them all under you."

Trepov, foiled in his plan to get rid of Protopopov, sent an emissary to Rasputin to offer an enormous bribe, a house and bodyguard and magnificent pension, if he would agree to dismiss Protopopov and refrain from interfering any further in government.

Rasputin laughed himself hoarse on hearing the offer.

"Out of my way!" he ordered the emissary. "I have other more urgent business to conduct with the little seamstress upstairs."

And flinging the envoy out unceremoniously, he bounded

up the stairs two at a time to the flat above. He had urgent need of her agile body to rid himself of all his accumulated tensions, and she had proved willing and able often enough in the past.

TWENTY-TWO

PRINCE FELIX YUSUPOV, darling of St Petersburg society, was ineffably bored. Born into a family with centuries of accumulated wealth and treasures, owning four palaces in St Petersburg alone as well as three in Moscow and thirty-seven estates all over Russia, he had been pampered all his life, graced by nature with extreme good looks and charm, and had sealed his cachet to popularity by a brilliant marriage. His beautiful young wife Princess Irina was a niece of the Tsar.

Fortune could not have favoured the young man more greatly. Owing to the death of his elder brother in a duel, Felix became heir to the vast estates and Fabergé art treasures, the gold plate and historic treasures heaped in the family's many mansions. He led a life of idle luxury, testing every form of sensual enjoyment from girls to opium, played at being a student, a dilettante and a playboy, but much as he was fawned upon and idolised, he could not find excitement. Even when war came, there was no military service for him. The life of bohemianism began to pall. Wealth and adulation had its drawbacks. There seemed to be no goal to strive for, for everything was already his. Felix Yusupov groaned in the most unspeakable boredom.

And he was heartily sick of the non-stop conversation in every St Petersburg salon about that peasant Rasputin. It was evident everyone loathed and feared the starets, but somehow they were fascinated by him, even gentle little Munia Golovina.

166

She and her mother had been hypnotised by Rasputin's ridiculous rhetoric for some years now, and were his ardent disciples.

"I do wish you would meet Father Gregory again," Munia would urge him plaintively. "I know you did not care for him when you first met, but I know he took a liking to you. Please, do let me ask you both to tea. I'm sure he could help you."

Felix resisted, politely but firmly. He did not wish to hurt Munia whom he knew had always had a soft spot for him in her heart, long before he married Irina. So he did not tell her how much the peasant's uncouth manners and brazen familiarity angered him, how he longed to punch the leathery, leering face when the old libertine gave both mother and daughter smacking kisses on the lips and caressed them. Munia and her mother regarded Rasputin as a saint who could do no wrong.

"I wish you could see him in his true light, as I do," Munia said sorrowfully. "Whatever blasphemies may be spoken of him, like Christ he ignores it and continues manfully. He is a holy man indeed."

Yusupov grunted and kept silent. He knew he was not alone in his hatred of the peasant upstart whose power had gone to his head, turning him into a man with a mania, a lust for even greater power. But it was only when he read in the newspaper a report of a speech by Purishkevich before the Duma, in which the deputy denounced Rasputin's dark forces, that his anger crystallised into determination.

"It requires only the recommendation of Rasputin to raise the most abject citizen to high office," the enraged deputy had roared to the Duma. "If you are truly loyal, if the glory of Russia . . . means anything to you, then on your feet, you ministers! Be off to Headquarters and throw yourself at the feet of the Tsar. Have the courage to tell him what the multitude is threatening in its wrath. Revolution threatens and an obscure moujik (Holy Man) shall govern Russia no longer."

The speech had gained tumultuous applause from the audience in the Duma, and Felix Yusupov felt the same angry glow rousing his spirit to action. Of course—that was what he sought—to do some challenging act that would give his sated life some purpose. Rid the country of this upstart tyrant!

A crime! Yes, that was one sensation Yusupov had never savoured. If he could commit, not just some petty crime, but the murder of a man so hated and feared as this starets—now that would be a sensation indeed! Yusupov's brainwave fascinated him, making the blood gallop through his veins as it had never done for a long, long time. He went to visit Purishkevich in a state of seething, feverish excitement, taking with him his close friend, the young Grand Duke Dimitri. Dimitri, a lieutenant in the Life Guards, was not only as handsome and rich and bored as himself, but he was also a member of the Royal Family, cousin to the Tsar. For him to be involved in ridding the country of Rasputin could only reflect honour on the much-reviled Royal Family, and help to restore their popularity.

Purishkevich was delighted to hear the two young men planned such a coup. The three men sat closeted, discussing the plan eagerly.

"We shall need help," Purishkevich suggested. "Two others at least. I propose we enlist the aid of Dr Lazovert, a trusted friend of mine."

"And Lieutenant Sukhotin," added Dimitri. "I know he will concur gladly."

So for the sake of secrecy, the conspirators met daily on a disused hospital train which was under Purishkevich's command.

"Secrecy is of the essence," said Yusupov, chafing his hands together as he spoke. The train was unheated, snow was falling outside, and the men shivered in their great coats and fur gloves. "He must disappear without trace, so that we may not be discovered."

"Poison him," Purishkevich suggested. "It is quiet, and then we can dispose of the body."

"But how do we administer it?" Dimitri queried. "How can we be certain it reaches him? Remember it has been tried before, and only his cat died."

"We must administer it personally," Lazovert stated calmly, "so there is no mistake. But there must be no witnesses."

"That's easier said than done," Dimitri murmured. "He's a wily fox. How do we lull him into feeling secure—how can we make the whole thing appear natural?"

"I know." Yusupov's voice was eager. "It can be done at my house. Munia Golovina has long been anxious to bring Rasputin and me together again—I shall let her do it! By her account, Rasputin was impressed by me and is anxious to meet me again, so I will appear to soften and let her effect the rapprochement!"

Voices murmured in consideration. "It will work, I know it will!" Yusupov's voice was growing shrill with excitement.

"In your own house?" queried Purishkevich, gazing out at the snow. "Yes, the fate of Russia is at stake, a stake too high for any personal consideration to count. So let it be. Now all that remains is to decide how to dispose of the body— completely—once the deed is done."

Earnest voices fell to discussing the details under the flicker of candlelight. Yusupov was to allow Munia to bring him and Rasputin together, to cultivate the starets' friendship, and eventually invite him to his home. Dr Lazovert, as an expert on poisons, was to determine the means they would use.

"But suppose Rasputin refuses to come to the palace? Suppose he finds some reason—tiredness, the bad weather or something—and will not come?" Dimitri suggested.

Purishkevich wagged his black-rimmed pince-nez at the youth. "He will not refuse if Felix says Irina is there. We all know Rasputin's predilection for beautiful women."

"My wife is away in the Crimea," Yusupov pointed out. "She will not be home till the New Year."

"Rasputin is not to know that. If you invite him to meet her and he thinks there is a chance he might convert her to his unholy faith, he will come to the palace, there is no doubt of that."

"And to make certain," Lazovert added finally, "I shall act the chauffeur and drive him by car to the palace myself. Will that satisfy your misgivings?"

Yusupov nodded contentedly. "And the body?"

Lazovert's eyes were sober. "I have thought of that. When he is poisoned, we will use the car to take him down to the river. A hole in the ice, dump the body in, and the swift current should carry him far away before he is found. No one can then connect it with us."

"Good idea," said Dimitri. "And you can use my car. With its insignia and the Grand Duke's pennant on the wing, no one will dare stop it and question its errand."

Purishkevich looked back at Yusupov. "Well, now it's up to you, Felix. Curry the fellow's favour and get him to your house. You will have to see to it that he takes the poison, but we will be in the house too, within call."

"You can safely leave it to me," Yusupov said with pride. At last he had a mission of real importance and a purpose in life which made it worth living again. "You can rely on me."

The men reached for their fur hats before facing the December blizzard outside, shook hands solemnly, and resolved to fix the date of the murder finally once the miscreant had been ensnared.

Not far away in a room in Gorovkhaya Street, the starets knelt before the ikon and prayed. He had been praying for hours for release from the terrible feeling of gloom and presentiment that enshrouded him, but without relief. Something terrible was going to happen, and soon, he knew it, but what it was and whence the blow would come he could not foresee. All he knew was that this awful foreboding had accompanied him everywhere since Purishkevich's denunciation. Only today as he walked down by the river Neva it had suddenly turned crimson before his eyes. He had told his secretary sadly on his return that the river was full of the blood of Grand Dukes, but why he had said it he did not know. A terrible prevision, perhaps? Revolution and the threat of bloodshed were undoubtedly in the air. God help the Tsar and Tsarina if ever revolution did come, for they would be the first to fall.

He had tried so hard to bolster the failing strength of the Crown. Russia had grown strong through her autocratic kings. If revolution came, bringing with it bloodshed and annihilation, Russia's path would never be the same again.

He bowed his head and prayed again. The air of heavy tension and oppression grew stronger. Rasputin sensed that if he looked upwards he would almost see the proverbial sword, hanging by a split hair, about to swoop on his head. It was final. It was irrevocable. His death must come, and soon.

Then, as he prayed, the startling vision came. He saw it all —panic, hunger, fear, riot, and death. Rivers of blood engulfed first himself and then countless more. Anarchy, ruin and terror prevailed.

The vision ended. Rasputin rose slowly and stiffly, and went to his desk. Taking out pen and paper and lighting the solitary candle, he began to write laboriously, a letter to be opened only after his death.

I write and leave behind me this letter at St Petersburg. I feel that I shall leave life before January 1. I wish to make known to the Russian people, to Papa (the Tsar), to the Russian Mother and the children, to the land of Russia, what they must understand.

If I am killed by common assassins, and especially by my brothers the Russian peasants, you, Tsar of Russia, have nothing to fear. Remain on your throne and govern . . . and you will have nothing to fear for your children. They will reign for hundreds of years in Russia.

But if I am murdered by boyars, nobles, and if they shed my blood, their hands will remain soiled with my blood. For twenty-five years they will not wash their hands from my blood. They will leave Russia. Brothers will kill brothers, and they will kill each other and hate each other, and for twenty-five years there will be no nobles in the country.

Tsar of the land of Russia, if you hear the sound of the bell which will tell you that Gregory has been killed, you must know this : if it was your relations who have wrought my death, then no one of your family, that is to say, none of your children or relations, will remain alive for more than two years. They will be killed by the Russian people.

I shall be killed. I am no longer among the living. Pray, pray, be strong, think of your blessed family.

Gregory.

He sighed heavily as he folded and sealed the letter. It was all true, he knew it as clearly as if he had seen it with his own eyes, for his inner vision had beheld it. Not only the young Tsarevitch would die without Rasputin's aid, but the lot of them.

And himself. He would be dead from some traitor's hand before the New Year came. And it was mid-December already.

TWENTY-THREE

LATE one night Rasputin walked home through the snow-slushed streets. Despite an evening of riotous drinking and swearing, dancing furiously and leaping on the tables of the elegant Yar restaurant, he still felt moody and miserable. No amount of diversion or heavy wine-drinking could cheer his depression. Odd, but he never became drunk at all nowadays. His stomach lining must have thickened so tremendously now that little had any effect on it, certainly not the vast quantities of wine he had consumed.

He trudged along moodily. The boulevard was in the smarter quarters and the houses that lined it elegant and fashionable. A carriage stood in the street outside one house, its coachman on the box huddled deep into his greatcoat and looking like a statue in his covering of frost and snow. Suddenly the house door opened. A middle-aged man in evening cape was bidding good night to his hostess.

"Good night, Sophie dear. Till Thursday then." He gave her a quick kiss and descended the steps. Rasputin stopped to watch. The gentleman brushed past him and called to the coachman.

"To the Villa Rode, Jakob. Make haste!"

The coachman did not move.

"You hear me, man! Doff your cap when I speak to you, you wretched peasant!" the gentleman exclaimed in irritation. His hostess stood watching curiously in the doorway.

"Dammit, I think the fellow's gone to sleep! I know I stayed for longer than I intended, but there's no need for him to go to sleep on the job. Wake up, you wretch, and get moving!"

The gentleman reached up and gave the driver a savage jab. As Rasputin watched, the driver's figure leaned over stiffly sideways, rolled and fell off the cab. The gentleman was startled.

"Good gracious, what's wrong with the fellow?" he exclaimed again, and bent to examine the prostrate figure. When he straightened, his lined face wore a look of utter disgust.

"Sophie, would you believe it! He's dead, frozen stiff! How inconsiderate, when I'm late for the others at the Villa Rode too!"

"No matter," the young woman's voice called from the doorway. "Wait a moment, and I'll lend you my coachman."

Rasputin watched, his grey eyes thoughtful. Within moments a new driver had been procured and the gentleman, smiling now, drove off to keep his appointment. Rasputin could see the horses' nostrils emitting huge bursts of steam in the lamplit air as they cantered away. The house door closed and the street became silent and deserted once more, save for Rasputin's watchful figure and the corpse in the gutter.

Rasputin went closer and bent over the body.

"So it is with all such as we, my friend. We are expendable to the boyars. But have no fear, your wrongs will be avenged. The people of Russia are girding their loins to attack. It will not be long."

Then he turned and continued to shuffle aimlessly along the pavement. There was no hurry to return to his bed. Sleeplessness and worry and an ever-present sense of doom were his bedmates nowadays. He worried ceaselessly about the Tsar and the Empress. As a peasant he, like all the others, recognised only the autocratic ruler as the head of Russia, for so it had been from time immemorial. The boyars were the villains, those who came between the Tsar and his loving people, but in their misery and anger the people would turn on Nicholas too when revolution came.

He was jerked out of his morbid thoughts by the sight of a woman's figure huddled against the wall outside his house, burying herself deep into her cloak against the bitter wind. Another one seeking help at this time of night? He approached and looked at her questioningly.

"Oh, Gregory! I'm so glad you've come! I've waited hours!"

It was Tanya. She was white, but whether with cold or with tension he did not know.

"Come inside. We can talk there."

"No—listen! You are watched all the time, but I had to come. Serge overheard something—he's in the guard, you know, and he overheard a conversation, in a train. There were ministers and boyars—they talked of killing you!"

Rasputin smiled. "No doubt that is a daily conversation nowadays in St Petersburg. You know how I am hated. But do not worry, Tanya."

"No—this was a genuine plot, Gregory. They plan to lure you to Prince Yusupov's palace and poison you! Serge told me. They plan to poison the cakes."

"Does Serge care about me, then?"

Tanya hung her head. "No, he believes the stories that are told about you, that you are a German spy and everything. He doesn't know I am here."

"Then why are you here, Tanya?"

She smiled shyly. "I am not ashamed to say it. I love you, Gregory. I have always loved you, since I was a little girl of twelve. I think you are a wonderful man, gifted with miraculous powers, and I am proud that I am your friend. That is why I came. They must not kill you, Gregory—oh, do say you won't go to the palace!"

Rasputin placed his hands on her shoulders and fixed her with his piercing grey eyes. "Tanya, my dear child, I am grateful to you. But your task is to care for your husband and child. As for me . . ." He shrugged and dropped his hands. "I shall be cared for. I am in God's hands, and who could be better placed? Thank you for coming, Tanya, and for your love and concern. Now go home, and God bless you."

Tanya's dark eyes searched his face for a moment hesitantly, then she nodded. "Very well, Gregory. May God bless and keep you, for Russia has need of a saint."

And she sped quickly away along the glistening street. Rasputin climbed the stairs wearily to his apartment. Odd that she had pinpointed Prince Yusupov as the source of the danger that threatened him, for he had come to like the young man immensely of late. They had met frequently in the last week or two at Madame Golovina's house, and Rasputin had believed that the prince had returned his genuine admiration. Felix Yusupov was a charming, talented fellow, singing gypsy songs to the accompaniment of his guitar, to Rasputin's great delight. Could Tanya—or Serge for that matter—have been mistaken? It seemed highly unlikely that the young prince could mean any harm to Rasputin. What reason could he possibly have?

It didn't make sense. Yusupov took no interest in politics, but he was married to the Tsar's beautiful niece Irina, so he must know how wholeheartedly Rasputin supported the monarchy. No, there must have been some mistake. True, Yusupov was now so amiably inclined towards Rasputin that he had invited him to his palace on the Moika, to meet the Princess Irina, but to Rasputin that only indicated the growing friendship between the two. True, the prince had suggested they keep the meeting a secret lest the Golovinas, mother and daughter, should be jealous of their idol's meeting with the beautiful Irina, but that had seemed sensible enough advice. Still, it wouldn't do any harm to take care. He could decline to eat while he was in the palace, and then he should be safe.

Having refuted the idea that his new friend could possibly be planning any treachery, Rasputin still could not sleep. The air of foreboding and precognition of doom would not leave him.

Anna Vyrubova called to see him the next afternoon. "I bring you a gift from the Empress," she said happily, unwrapping an ikon from a paper parcel.

Rasputin thanked her and went on to talk of his friendship with Yusupov.

"I am to visit him at the Moika Palace at midnight tonight to meet Irina," he told her.

Anna's eyebrows rose, but she made no comment. But alone with the Empress that evening, she mentioned the visit. Alexandra looked surprised.

"Yes, I thought it was an unseemly hour to go visiting," said Anna, seeing the look. "But I said nothing. It was not my place."

"To meet Irina, you said?" the Empress repeated in surprise. "But there must be some mistake. Irina is in the Crimea."

"Well, that's what he said."

"I see. But there must be some mistake," Alexandra repeated thoughtfully, then she dismissed it quickly from her mind and began another of her endless letters to her husband.

Rasputin prepared carefully for his visit to the Moika Palace, for it was not often one had the chance to meet someone of Irina's legendary beauty and charm. For once, he washed himself well with cheap soap that gave off a fierce

178

sweet smell and then dressed in his black velvet trousers and new leather boots, and pulled on his newest silk tunic embroidered with cornflowers. Then he tied a cord of red silk about his waist. There was still half an hour to go to midnight, when Yusupov promised the chauffeur would call for him. Rasputin lay on the fox fur bedspread and stared up at the ceiling, deep in thought.

Was Tanya right? Was there really any threat to his safety in this visit? Even Protopopov had today expressed his distrust of the situation, and warned Rasputin that he feared an attack on his friend's life. In view of Yusupov's friendly manner of late and his pressing invitation to come and meet Irina, it seemed unlikely that he meant harm, and Rasputin prided himself that he was rarely wrong in his assessment of a man. Could he have been deluded by the frank young face and clear soft eyes with their long lashes? There was such a tender, feminine air about the young man, some fifteen years his junior, that it was difficult to reconcile treachery with his open, honest face.

Rasputin sighed and stretched. He felt intolerably old and tired, and yet he was only forty-four years of age, the time when a man was supposedly in the full prime and vigour of his life. Alongside the youthful beauty of Yusupov he felt like Methuselah.

Young Felix. Rasputin recalled again the smiling face and open arms of his friend. He had so much in life, this boy— riches, popularity, a lovely wife and his whole life of luxury ahead of him. Could he be a dissembler? Could he have any reason to want to harm Rasputin? The more he considered it, the more Rasputin was convinced Tanya was mistaken. A few chance words overheard through a closed door could easily be misinterpreted. Serge had heard Rasputin's name mentioned —but who in St Petersburg did not discuss the powerful

179

influence on the throne these days? And he had heard the word poison—well, planning a murder was not so unusual in the atmosphere of rife intrigue in the city either.

Murder. Rasputin contemplated the idea. Whatever might have been attributed to him in the way of sin, that was one crime he had never committed. Whatever his manipulations, he had never caused anyone's death, though he might be branded as a libertine, a satyr, a fraud, a charlatan and even a spy, but no one ever suggested he could kill. It was strange, really, how differently people saw him. To half the world he was a beneficent starets, a man who could do no wrong because his voice was the voice of God, and to the rest he was the incarnation of evil itself. He laughed aloud, but there was no amusement in the sound. How could they hold such opposite views, and not one of them understand the real man, the bewildered creature seeking God and acting only on His revelations?

Praskovie understood. For all her limitations, she had been the one person who had understood his need and left him free to go and search for God. What a patient soul she was! He thought fondly of his family for a moment, the poor sickly son Dimitri and the two fine healthy girls, now well on the way to womanhood. Maria was here now, at school in St Petersburg. He only hoped that the animosity directed against him would not envelop her too.

The sound of bells on a droshka outside disturbed his reverie, and Rasputin rose from the bed slowly and crossed to the window. The car would be here soon now. In the shadows across the street he could see no sign of lurking, furtive figures, but he guessed the Ochrana would not be far away. His enemies kept note of his every move.

But not Felix. No, certainly he could not list young Yusupov amongst his enemies, he felt sure. He should be looking forward to this visit, to meeting the delectable Irina at last. A car glided quietly to a halt outside. Rasputin turned from the window and picked up his fur hat and coat. With determination he forced the black mood out of his heart and went down to open the door to the chauffeur.

TWENTY-FOUR

YUSUPOV met Rasputin eagerly at the door and led him downstairs to a cellar room. It was low-vaulted and had a stone floor, but the walls were papered and the room handsomely furnished. Bearskin and Persian rugs lay scattered over the floor and by the subdued light of the hanging lamps and the glow from the fire Rasputin could see the table laid for six, with wine and glasses and chocolate cake and biscuits, and on a silver tray a huge samovar.

Rasputin rubbed his hands together before the fire and surveyed the cosy scene. From upstairs came the sound of music.

"What's that?" he asked Yusupov. "Is there a party upstairs?"

"Irina is entertaining some friends," the young man replied smoothly. "Once they have left, she will join us. She did not want to share you with the others. Will you have some wine while we are waiting?"

Rasputin declined. "I should prefer tea."

"Very well." Yusupov poured out the golden liquid and handed it to Rasputin, then pushed the plate of chocolate cake towards him. Rasputin shook his head. Was it his imagination, or did young Yusupov's hand tremble, ever so slightly, as he handed Rasputin the glass of tea?

Rasputin shook the thought out of his mind. He was letting Tanya's fear contaminate him, playing tricks with his imagination. On second thoughts, he would have a piece of cake.

He reached for a slice of the chocolate cake and pushed

it into his mouth. It was remarkably sweet. Rather pleasant, in fact. He reached for a second slice.

Yusupov was looking at him closely, and there were tiny droplets of sweat on his smooth brow. Rasputin leaned forward.

"I feel . . ."

"Yes?" Yusupov's voice was sharp and questioning, and his eyes searching.

"I feel it must be very hot in here, for you are sweating, my friend."

"It is nothing. A glass of wine will cool me. Will you join me?"

He held the bottle of madeira aloft invitingly. Rasputin nodded. As the prince poured out two glasses the strains of the gramophone music upstairs soared and swelled.

"That's an American tune, isn't it?" Rasputin asked as he picked up the wine and tossed it off.

"Yes. 'Yankee Doodle Dandy'," Yusupov replied, and he refilled Rasputin's glass to the brim.

"Can't say I like it—not like our own Russian music." Rasputin tossed off the second glass. Then he noticed Yusupov's strange expression, the fixed, glazed look that came into his clear blue eyes. Maybe the wine was having the same effect on him as on himself, for he too felt slightly dizzy. Odd, for wine never affected him nowadays.

"More tea, to clear my head, Felix," he asked, "and then play to me on your guitar and delight me with your gypsy songs. I love to hear you sing."

"Gladly," the youth replied, and picking up the guitar he began to strum. Rasputin recognised the tune. It was one he loved, a gay, lively song. He threw back his head and joined in the song lustily. When it was ended, Yusupov looked at him enquiringly.

"Go on, go on," Rasputin urged. "Don't stop."

Several songs they sang together, and then Rasputin fell silent and pushed his glass forward. There was silence from the room upstairs now.

"More wine, Felix. My throat is dry from singing, and there is a bitter taste in my mouth."

Yusupov poured the wine without speaking and then rose and began to wander about the room, toying with an ivory figure on the red granite fireplace. He seemed to waver as he walked. Was the fellow becoming drunk already, or was it Rasputin's own eyes which, blurred by drink, could not focus properly? It was odd, decidedly odd.

The sound of footsteps upstairs came to Rasputin's ears.

"What is that?" he asked sharply.

Yusupov turned from the fireplace quickly. "I don't know. Perhaps my wife's guests are leaving at last. I'll go and see."

Rasputin watched his lithe young figure leave the room. What an amiable creature he was, young Felix! He glanced at the clock. Half past two already. He was beginning to feel very sleepy. If he was not careful Irina would find him fast asleep here on the couch when she eventually came down. He must try to keep awake. God, but his throat was hot!

Yusupov re-entered the room but remained standing near the door. His hands were clasped behind his back. After a moment he crossed the thick rug noiselessly and sat down opposite Rasputin. Rasputin watched him hazily, but had not the strength to raise his tired head from his chest where it had sunk.

"Do you not feel well?" Yusupov asked him at length. "You are breathing heavily."

"A little tired and my throat burns," Rasputin answered. He sat up with an effort and poured himself more wine. "In a moment I shall be myself again, and then . . ."

"And then?" Yusupov echoed, but his voice sounded far away.

"And then we shall pay a visit to the gypsies, eh? Now don't look offended," he added, seeing the look of surprise on the younger man's face. "With God in thought, but mankind in the flesh, eh?" He chuckled at the joke and winked meaningfully, but the chuckle hurt his throat. He watched blearily as Yusupov wandered away, across to the ebony cabinet in the corner. The prince fingered the heavy rock crystal crucifix that stood on it and seemed to be lost in thought.

"Do you like my crucifix, Gregory?" he asked in a distant voice. "It is crystal and silver, a very fine example of sixteenth-century Italian workmanship. Do you like it?"

Rasputin focused his bleary eyes on it with difficulty. He rose stiffly and crossed to have a closer look. Then his gaze travelled down to the cabinet below, magnificently inlaid with mirrors and little bronze columns.

"Your crucifix is very fine, Felix, but I like your cabinet better."

Yusupov fixed him with a strange look. "Father Gregory, you'd far better look at the crucifix and say a prayer." His tone was low and menacing. Rasputin looked up in surprise, to hear a voice so strange and inimical from his young friend. Yusupov's eyes were cold and intense. Rasputin met his look with one of equal strength and determination, a look which had quelled and mesmerised many in the past, but the prince's eyes did not waver. Rasputin felt a sudden stab of apprehension. He turned back to look at the crucifix.

At the very moment that he looked away he heard a deafening crash and felt a searing pain in his back, an agonising, rending, burning pain. He heard the roar that issued from his own lips, and then fell backwards through an eddying black mist.

185

Yusupov stared down at the great figure sprawled on the white bearskin rug in fascination. He had done it! At last, the poison having failed, he had shot the devil! Exultation throbbed in his veins. In the two-and-a-half agonising hours alone with the wretch he had begun to fear that he would never die, for neither poisoned cake nor poisoned wine had seemed to affect him. But now, thank God, the peasant was done for.

Purishkevich and Sukhotin and Lazovert rushed in. "We heard the shot!" Purishkevich exclaimed. "Ah, thank God," he added, seeing the body on the floor.

Lazovert knelt and took Rasputin's pulse. "He is dead," he pronounced. "Remarkably little bleeding. The bullet must have penetrated his heart. Let us remove the body from the white rug, however, lest bloodstains should incriminate us."

Purishkevich helped him drag the heavy figure across to the door, where they left it lying on the stone flags.

"Now for the car," said Lazovert. "Sukhotin, take Rasputin's coat and hat and put them on. I shall drive you to the Gorokhovaya, and then we can dump his things. If he has been trailed, that will put them off the scent. Quickly, switch off the light, Sukhotin."

Sukhotin did so, and the three men went out. Yusupov continued to stare at the burly, ugly figure on the floor with inexpressible disgust. In the flickering light from the fire he looked even more vile and evil than in life. It had been too easy, really. One could hardly believe that evil of such force could be cut off so simply.

He shuddered. The treacherous thought kept insinuating itself into his mind that the beast might not be dead, but only shamming, or that the powers of evil might help him in some obscure way to recover. To reassure himself, Yusupov touched the body. It was still warm, but so was the cellar room. He lifted the arms and head, but they sank lifelessly to the floor again.

What an incredulous, superstitious fool he was being, behaving more like the ignorant, unlearned peasant he despised than an intelligent aristocrat! Nevertheless, he would be glad when Lazovert and Sukhotin returned from laying their false trail, and they could get this vile creature out of his house.

Yusupov paced anxiously about the cellar, then came back to look at the corpse. Without warning, one heavy eyelid slowly opened and Rasputin's face twitched. Yusupov recoiled in horror. Then both eyes, green and menacing in the firelight, opened and stared at him with an expression of diabolical hatred.

He stood motionless, rooted to the spot in terror. The body moved, sat up and then suddenly leapt to its feet, foam massing at the mouth. Rasputin lunged forward at him, trying to tear at his throat, and Yusupov felt the epaulette on his shoulder being ripped off. The scream locked in his throat burst out, he dashed away the powerful hands that tore at him, and fled. Screaming and scrambling on all fours, he ran up the stairs, calling for Purishkevich, for he had taken the pistol. He was frantic with terror, the lumbering figure of Rasputin close behind him.

"Purishkevich! Fire, fire! He's getting away!" Yusupov shrieked, and almost collided with Purishkevich's portly figure at the head of the stairs. Thrusting him aside, Yusupov fled into the safety of his parents' apartment. Once inside, he locked the door and sank slowly down the doorpost.

Purishkevich clutched the pistol, fascinated by the sight of the great figure which clambered up the steps and hurled its weight against the door leading out into the courtyard, bursting it open, and stumbling out blindly into the night. Purishkevich followed, but was too terrified to venture outside. The huge figure of Rasputin was lumbering across the courtyard to the gate, his great voice bellowing and filling the icy air.

"Felix! Felix! I will tell everything to the Empress!" the bull-like voice roared.

Purishkevich's frightened finger tightened on the trigger. All would be lost if the Tsarina came to hear of it.

Two shots rang out, but the burly shape blundered on, nearing the gate. At the third shot he halted and clutched his shoulder. Purishkevich shook with terror, bit his left hand to make himself concentrate, and fired again. Rasputin sank to the ground. Purishkevich ran up to the inert figure, kicked it hard on the temple, and saw Rasputin lie still, only his teeth grinning. Apart from the teeth there was little else visible in the face, for it had been badly shattered. Purishkevich realised the fourth bullet must have hit him in the head.

He kicked the body again, and Yusupov, who appeared suddenly from out of the house, began belabouring it with a truncheon, but this time there was no reaction. The devil was decidedly dead.

"I have killed him," Purishkevich murmured in disbelief and then, exultation starting to fill his body, "I have killed Grishka Rasputin, the enemy of Russia and the Tsar," he cried aloud.

Lazovert and Dimitri and Sukhotin returned and helped wrap the body in a blue curtain, tie it with rope and drive it to the river. They cut a hole in the ice and pushed their bundle in, but in their haste and anxiety they overlooked one of Rasputin's boots which lay, forlorn and neglected, on the ice.

TWENTY-FIVE

YUSUPOV's explanation of the shots heard in his courtyard, that a wild party had culminated in one of his guests shooting a dog, did not delude the Empress at all. Despite her fears over Rasputin's disappearance, she firmly ordered him and Dimitri to be placed under close house-arrest, and later Yusupov was sent away to one of his country estates. Dimitri was sent to the Persian front, and Purishkevich was allowed to continue his hospital work at the front.

Morbid fear for her holy friend now possessed the Empress. She languished in her mauve boudoir, surrounded by flowers and the scent of burning incense, and wrote anxiously to her husband.

Our Dear Friend has disappeared . . . Yesterday Anna saw him and he said Felix asked him to come in the night . . . This night big scandal at Yusupov's house— big meeting, Dimitri, Purishkevich, etc., all drunk; police heard shots, Purishkevich ran out screaming . . . that Our Friend was killed . . .

Our Friend was in good spirits but nervous these days. Felix pretends he never came to the house. . . . I shall still trust in God's mercy that one has only driven him away somewhere . . . I cannot and won't believe that he has been killed. God have mercy. Such utter anguish . . . Come quickly.

Three days later the body of Rasputin was found. The bloodstained boot had given the clue to searchers, and they found the corpse below the ice. His lungs were full of water, and there were claw marks under the ice, and the right hand was freed from the rope, indicating that he was still alive when he was pushed under. Rasputin's daughters Maria and Varvara were summoned to identify the body of their father, and the corpse taken to the chapel of a veterans' home at Chesma, half-way between St Petersburg and Tsarskoe Selo.

People rejoiced openly in the streets that the beast was dead, acclaiming Yusupov and his confederates as saviours. Only the peasants further afield mourned the passing of a saint, and the bitterly lonely Empress Alexandra.

The New Year, 1917, was just dawning as they laid him to rest in the Imperial Park. As he had prophesied, he did not live beyond the year's end. The sun shone on a sparkling world of crisp snow and crystalline ice, and the sleigh bells of the few mourners sounded his funeral knell on the hushed air.

The royal party stood at the graveside. Anna Vyrubova wept openly, but the Empress stood pale and composed, clutching a bunch of white flowers. She was thinking of the staret's promise, that she and her family would be safe so long as he lived and of his terrible prophecy, "If I die, the Tsar will soon after lose his Crown." And now he was gone. What did the future hold for her beloved ones now? God have mercy on us, she prayed in anguish, and dear Father Gregory watch over us. She thought of the words in the note she had had placed on his breast inside the coffin.

My dear martyr, give me thy blessing that it may follow me always on the sad and dreary path I have yet to follow here below. And remember us from on high in your holy prayers.

Alexandra.

The service was over. She distributed the flowers she carried among her daughters and friends and watched them scatter the blooms on the oak coffin. Then she turned sadly away and went back to the royal car. She did not notice the young woman in common clothes at the gate as she drove past.

"It is over," the young woman said to her husband, taking his arm and sighing deeply. "He is gone. I feel sorry for the Tsarina now, for he was so kind to her."

"Come now, Tanya," her husband remonstrated as they walked away. "He was the devil incarnate, and well you know it, playing on a feeble woman so and trying to run Russia as if he were the Tsar himself."

"He was a good man, Serge."

"So you have always said, but one's childhood memories of people can be misleading, you know. Just because you came from the same village is no reason to idolise him. No, he was a fraud, Tanya, pretending to be a holy man when all the time he was a scheming, lecherous villain. The world is well rid of him, if you ask my opinion."

"He was a saint," Tanya breathed softly. "A veritable saint. The world will never see his like again, I fear."

Serge snorted and drew her arm firmly through his. The snow was still sparkling under the sunlight as they retraced their steps towards the city, but Tanya could find no joy in its beauty. Somehow, despite the scintillating crispness of the day, there hung a vague presentiment, a sense of foreboding in the air that cast a gloom over the sunlit snow. It was an uneasy feeling of trouble yet to come, a hint of bloodlust in the air, and Tanya could only wonder and sigh deeply. Something was to come of it yet. The repercussions of Rasputin would still be felt in Russia. What would the poor Tsarina do without him?

Ah well, it was no use talking to Serge about it. He would

only laugh at her vague, badly-phrased misgivings and urge her to think of what was for supper instead. She smiled up at her husband, and hoped that now that the Tsar was home from the front, he too would be able to comfort his sad wife.

Little was Tanya to know that within a year the Tsar, the Empress and their children would be lying in a cellar in Ekaterinburg, awaiting their deaths from assassins' bullets. In the revolution that followed many had occasion to recall the prophet's words :

"I see many tortured creatures, whole masses of people, great heaps, crowds of bodies! Among them are many grand dukes and hundreds of counts. The Neva will be red with blood!"